Mind Games

A

Novel

By

KaShamba

Williams

Advanced Praise for
Mind Games

"A great new read from one of the pioneers of the street game."
- **Carl Weber,** New York Times Best selling Author/ President of Urban Books

"She's back! KaShamba Williams' new book is mind blowin'! A must have for any 'real' reader of urban novels!"
- **Shannon Holmes**, Legendary Urban Fiction Author, B-More Careful, Bad Girlz, Dirty Game,

"KaShamba has once again proven herself a legitimate force in an over saturated industry."
- **K'Wan** international best selling author of Gangsta, Street Dreams, Hood Rat and Blow

"The wind has blown in a different direction in this street lit game and behind the powerful breeze is vet, KaShamba Williams. Not only is this strong gust going to blow out the competition, but it's going to blow your mind as well! Mind Games is the most skillfully crafted literary work in Mrs. William's arsenal to date. This is one brain trip you don't want to miss."
- **JOY**- *ESSENCE Magazine* bestselling author of *Mama, I'm in Love with a Gangsta*.

"A beautiful mind wrote Mind Games, once again KaShamba has crafted a novel that's worthy of Literary Hood certification."
- **Brandon McCalla**, Author of the Diamond Drought, Diamond Dynasty, Spot Rushers & Street Fiction

"KaShamba Williams, the vicious villain with a pen continues to write hot and steamy novels and with Mind Games, she's done it again!"
- **Reginald L. Hall**, aka The Prince of Gay Literature & Essence Best Selling novel of Memoir Delaware County prison and In Love with a Thug.

"Mind Games is filled with extreme drama, suspense and intrigue."
- **Hickson,** Publisher of Convict's Candy & Harder and Author of GhettoHeat & Skate On

"Serenity Wells is the reason men don't trust women period! She's worse than a good girl gone bad."
- **Mark Anthony,** Publisher of Q'Boro Books, Author of Harlem Heat, The Take Down & Lady's Night

This book is a work of fiction. Names, characters, place and incidents are results of the author's imagination or are used fictitiously. Any resemblance to locations, actual events or persons, living or dead is entirely coincidental.

Precioustymes Entertainment
229 Governors Place, #138
Bear, DE 19701
www.precioustymes.com

Library of Congress Control Number: 2006906672
ISBN# 0-9776507-2-3
         978-0-9776507-2-9
Editor: Joanie Smith
Proofreader: Crystal Gamble-Nolden
Cover Design/Graphics: candacek

First Trade Paperback Edition Printing July 2007
Printed in United States

Dedication

Sometimes, I stall writing another book because it seems like every time a new book of mine releases, someone very dear to me has passed on.

To Pop-Pop
Hewitt Bundy, Jr. aka Sonny (R.I.P.)

It's still hard to believe that you've crossed over. I hold no regrets. One thing I know is for sure you knew how much I loved you. Many have complained that I was your favorite grandchild. I beg to differ. You loved us all the same. I just happen to stand out more. ☺ I love you Pop-Pop and I will always keep our memories in my heart.

To my Great Grandfather aka Granddad
George Foster (R.I.P. Quiet Storm)

From the moment I was able to understand the meaning of a true father, you had already set the tone. When your partner (my great grandmother) died not long after she gave birth to your twins, you never hesitated to fill the void they had. From your example, any man bred from the Foster family should be a prime example that Black men are excellent fathers.

To cousin Jimmae Washington (R.I.P.)

It's amazing how you can know someone and not realize how astounding they are/were. I knew you were an amazing woman, but I didn't realize how truly remarkable you were until your untimely death.
May your life continue to shine through others!
Spread your wings Ma Mae.

To my son – Lil' Bobby (R.I.P.)

I see you smiling down on me. Your mother has come a long way. I thank God for allowing me to share the time you were here on earth. He sent you to change my life and what a change was made. All praise due to God!

Acknowledgments

To my Lord and Savior, I can't thank you enough for revising and revitalizing my life!

To my husband Lamotte, can you forgive me for being so selfish this go 'round?

To my babies, with each moment I thank God for allowing me to be apart of your lives. You keep me aligned.

To my mom, my #1 fan. Here's another to add to your brag rights.

To my brother Kenyatta, I'm so proud of you for moving forward. Treat Wanda like the Queen she is.

To my cousin Kashamba Busby (Purple Heart recipient) God has a plan for you. If it were meant for you to die in Iraq, it would've happened. But it didn't. Live life without regrets. I'm proud of you, cousin.

Mom Nita (R.I.P), Aunt Alice (R.I.P), Grandmom Florine (R.I.P.).

Dad and Dee, although, I don't come around, it doesn't mean I love you any less.

Grandmom Portia, Leslie, Alexis, Toni, Bonita, Malik, Aunt Robin, Granddad, Kenny, Angie, Aunt Paulette, Kim, Steven, my step-daughter Jasmine, my step-son Lamotte, Kendra, Rhythm, Lois Moore, Teali, Brown (Do the time, don't let the time, do you), Hank, Bop, Nap, Aunt Tootie, Tuesday, Janice, Hodgey, Rhonda, Uncle Edward, Uncle David, Donald, Shontia, Cartilla, Tish, Ronnika, Kimyatta,

Ms. Almethar, Uncle Mike, Aunt Ethel, Candy, Bobby Gibbs – Keep ya' head up! Carlton, Pete.

To all my nieces and nephews – Aunt Rae loves you!

To the H.E.I.C. – Head Editor in Charge – Joanie Smith, I don't know who's more stubborn, you or I. I almost did this without you. Let's not let that happen anymore. We work well together. I promise to stop slacking. ☺

To Crystal Gamble-Nolden bka Nardsbaby, Connoisseur of the written word – you know you the truth. Yes, I said it like that ☺. Thanks for saving me the headaches. You know you have a position with PTE, right?

To all the dedicated readers that support KaShamba Williams, the author, and Precioustymes Entertainment, without you, we wouldn't exist. Thank you!

To fellow Authors & Publishers

It's been a journey for all of us. Those that are still standing I continue to salute you! Al Saadiq Banks, Shannon Holmes, Vickie Stringer, K'Wan, Mark Anthony, Hickson, Brandon McCalla, Jo-Jo – you can handle the headaches, I can't, Shahida Fennel, Leondrei Prince, Treasure Blue, Mark Anthony, Denise Campbell, William Cooper, Corey Miller (C-Murder), Reginald Hall, Joylynn Jossel, T.N. Baker, Tracy Brown, Danielle Santiago, Eric Gray. To my brothas on lockdown doing something positive now and writing best selling novels to occupy their time - K'wame Teague, Leo Sullivan, Darrell Debrew, and Victor Martin. To Jason Poole, Jaeyel, Trustice, Azarel, Heather Covington, Shawna Grundy, Jessica Tilles, Ralph Johnson, Nishawnda, Ki-Ki Swinson, Anna J, Reshonda Billings-Tate, Kendra Bellamy, Eric Pete, Crystal Lacey-Winslow, Dorothy Goines, J.M. Benjamin – you hustle hard, Thomas Long – the movie

4Life is a GREAT look, congrats! Jihad, Alisha Yvonne, Deborah Smith, and N'tyse.

PTE Authors

Lenaise Meyeil – Stay creative. I'm proud of you. Stiletto 101 was a great read, but Vendetta: Diary of a Kingpin's Daughter is even better. Unique J. Shannon – May you prosper and continue to create entertaining stories. G. Rell – Study the game. Don't make sudden moves and you will prosper. B.P. Love – Will Latin Heat ever come out? Can you stop rewriting it? Tony Trusell – Still patiently waiting, I know. I promise you, One Love 'Til I Die will release this year. Brittney Davis -In My Peace I Trust, that's a model that I live by (peace). Stay humble and focus on your craft. Tracy Gray-Caruthers, as a reader myself, I loved Thug's Passion! Latifa Sanchez, welcome to the family! A special shout out to Joel "Dolo" Rhodes and Tasha. Keep God first, stay positive and learn from your mistakes. Remember, God will make a way out of no way!

To the Literary Heads

Precioustymes yahoo group, C2C Readers, Real Divas of Literature, Hakeem/Black & Nobel books – Thank you, bro. Mejah Bookstore, Emlyn, Marilyn, Diane, Jewel and Carmen. Ninth Street Books, Borders Express, B&N's, Waldenbooks, Shrine of the Black Madonna, Darryl Harris, Source of Knowledge, Expressions, Urban Knowledge, Sepia & Sable, Truth, Tru Books, Karibu, Robilyn Heath, Karen, Stephanie, Tiff & Zyaire, A&B, Afrikan World, Masaamba in Queens, Liquorous, Tiffany Elliott – thank you for your help, DC Bookman, Khalil, Malik, and many more. Angie Henderson – Adeeva Publicity, Raw Sistazs Reviewers, Yasmine – APOOO, OOSA Online Bookclub, A Nu Twistaflavah, Forefront magazine, LIVE magazine, The Grits, Heather Covington – Disigold magazine, Ebony

Expressions, Mahogany bookclub, Sister2Sister, Lloyd & Kevin (Boston, MA) www.theblacklibrary.com, AALBC, Go On Girl, ARC, Amorous Sepia Readin Sistahs, Sistah Circle, Ebony Eyes, Between Friends and to all the other clubs that read any of my books – thank you!

Special Shouts

To my on again/off again close friends, LOL! Donza, Tiffany, Cheryl, Wink, Nieka, Saundra and Larae. Y'all know I still love y'all.

To my lil' sis and Godsister – Cabrella, you are always there when I need you, girl.

Armelvis Booker – thank you for being you! Continue to pay it forward. Cindy – congrats on the new marriage! Ella, Autumn, Devon Chambers, Mil, Martina Gibbs, Shana, Shay, Tammy, Nicole, Shawn, Dawn, Cabrella, Russell, Ada, Michelle, Kita, Charmaine, Helen, Terrance, Keisha, Red, Ronnie & Timmy, Ms. Francine, Buddha, Brian, Darren, Randy, Squirt, Rhonda, Renee, Chalary, Mrs. Lois, Ronnie, Gayle, Sheen, Karen, Dee-Dee, Shawn, Demar, Deartis, Shell, Bryon, Raven, Theresa, Robyn, Will, Cheryl Brothers, Poo, Lill, Professor Hurdle, Detective Mayfield, Detective Chapman. The real Medina and Serenity. Nashya and Shawn. Tanya and Mark, Roslyn and Billy. Curtis Demby, Ja'Maal Oglesby, Melissa, Kiana, Will, Rob Berry, Keith Brown, Spoony, Doug, Mike, Kitty, Black, Melanie, Verna, Simone, Linda, Tina, Tracy, Tilla, Roslyn, Elgin Carrington, Duvowel, Crystal – All God's Children, Kevin Carr – Ocj Graphix, Foster's, Williams', Carrington's, Redden's, Ross' Gibbs', Armstead's, Moore's, to everyone holding me down...

Special shout out to Teneishae Coleman, Tronda, Shenetta, Bud, Barbara and to all of the other models that have graced my covers and PTE's covers.

Also to Salem City, Regina Gatson, Mrs. Jetter, David, Boone, Miss Pitts, Simone, Tweety, Tasha, Pop, Marcus, James Spain, Marquis, OG Cliff Montana, Tacarlfree, Jasmine, Angel and so many more.

Hold up, I can't forget the former staff of Urban Knowledge DE (Christiana Mall), Naya, LeCole, Richard, Tiffany, Carmen, and Jasmine. Thank you for putting in long hours to make the store a success! And, putting up with me ☺.

Thank you Percy Miller (Master P) for the revelation. I'm looking forward to working with you.

To anyone I missed please accept my apology.

I'd love to hear your comments.
Visit me online at www.KaShambaWilliams.com
Or, email me at kashamba@precioustymes.com.

If you've ever been in a "situation" and have been untrustworthy, this story is for you.

If you're currently in a relationship and are being deceitful and untrue, this story is for you.

If for years, you've put up with a man's bullshit because security is involved, this story is for you.

If for years, you've put up with a woman's bullshit because security is involved, this story is for you.

If you've ever connected with a man and the sex was that damn good, you didn't care if he had a woman at home, this story is for you.

If you've ever connected with a woman and the sex was so blazin' you overlooked that she had a man, this story is for you.

With that said if you fit into one of these categories, I have two questions to ask you... What lie are you telling yourself to stay? And, when are you going to get real with yourself and be true to you?

At the end of the day, you have to look yourself in the mirror.

Enjoy the read,
KaShamba

Mind Games

Pandora's Box – myths are this box is filled with secrets, deceit, evil thoughts and wrongdoings.

What's My Mothafuck'n Name?

My mother named me Serenity because I was the calm before the storm in her abusive relationship with my Pop. Bitches most definitely be hatin' too – mad that they don't have a fly-ass name like mine. My shit is very much original... and no; it's not a nickname. It's on some real shit. However, as surreal as I made my mother feel, for myself and others, I brought the ruckus! It's not anything peaceful, tranquil or serene about my trifling ass. Yes, I admit it. The first step to recovery is to admit that you have a problem; so let me be the first to admit it. My name is Serenity and I am an addict to hood life! This is not the typical story of a Hustler's Wife – hell nah! Hustler's wives are weak, broke down fragile bitches. I'm what you call a Hustle Bunny. We get down for ours when our man has done us wrong, na'mean. Fuck niggas, get money!

I am the daughter that you regret having. The kind of girl your grandmother warned you about. The little sister you want to beat down. The older sister you're ashamed of and refuse to look up to. The baby momma you don't want to have raising your kids. The sneaky girl next door you might catch creepin'. The girlfriend that you know is cheating, but you can't prove it. That best friend that you're tired of lying for to save her ass. I am the cousin that you love to hang around because you know we're about to have a blast, but before the end of the night get in some shit. I'm that real chick that you know you can count on (50% of the time), and most of all... the girlfriend you don't wanna have when you go to jail because you know my ass ain't gon' be faithful! Yep, that's me. And, I love every bit of who I am! Sometimes it's a blessing... and a curse. But I am still Ella's child. ☺

In a Flash

You know how you react impulsively and regret that shit after you've compromised yourself? Well, that's the point that I'd arrived to. I didn't mean to fuck up my life as bad as I had, but I did.

"Serenity, Serenity, is you with me?" Medina's voice (my best friend) flashed through my mind. I was too consumed by my new surroundings. My situation had become f-'d up! Trust me when I tell you it was extremely fucked up! Seems like last night the shit all went down...

The wind in the car blew directly in my face flapping my hair from my head to my cheekbones. The breeze was needed. Here I was mad as fuck! My underarms were perspiring and I could smell my pear scented Secret deodorant working overtime. My upper lip was sweaty and my forehead was beaded with moisture. I'm staring at the man that I gave whole-heartedly (well, in a sense) twelve mothafuck'n years of my life – good years too, and I hate his ass with a passion. In disgust, my head drooped between my breast that appeared to be getting juicer and plumper by the month. I don't know if it was because of the weight gain or from my man sucking them for his daily nourishment. My breasts were never close to a 38DD. Now, every bra I purchased was in that size. I wanted to say to Kyron, my man for ten years, but my husband for two years – *fuck you*!

I knew I shouldn't have married him in the first place after the nigga took ten years to propose. But, I couldn't fix my mouth to say, "No," when the bastard asked me to be his wife. I looked back at the innocent faces of my daughters, ages 7 and 4, and knew it would've been dead wrong to disrespect him in their presence. I promise you though, when I have a chance to get that nigga to myself, it's gonna be the rematch of Oscar Delahoya –vs- Pretty Boy Floyd Mayweather in this bitch!

The sweat was pouring down my face and each chance we got; I made sure we stopped to get ice-cold water to cool us down. It had to be at least 98 degrees with 95% humidity. My hair wrap was no longer straight and silky; it was more wet and wavy from the extensive heat. The air conditioning needed to be charged in the rusty ass 1986 GMC Safari van I'm forced to ride in. A bitch used to sit pretty in a factory waxed Excursion sitting on 22's. Imagine that! Now, I'm flexing in this old hooptie. What the fuck I look like – soccer mom? And the truth is, we are barely on a set of wheels. This damn van keeps breaking the fuck down and every time it does, I think less and less of my husband. I was heaving so hard in resentment and I knew this nigga could feel the heat coming from my nostrils. Yet, he's playing with the tape deck – yeah, a mothafuck'n tape deck. We don't even have a portable C.D. player in this piece of shit and he's trying to rewind crying, begging-ass, Gerald Levert (may he R.I.P.). I wanted to call my girl Medina to tell her about this shit, but my cell phone ran out of minutes. Yeah, a bitch had to stoop that low and get a damn prepaid.

My husband caught a case back in '02 and came out three years later. I was faithful to him the first year he was down. I'm not saying that I didn't jump off on him when he was home. I'd be lying if I said I didn't. For years I was faithful to him. It wasn't until he cheated on me first that I even considered getting him back.

Back in the day, I was a dedicated girlfriend and the only guy that took my world for a spin was Kyron. However, when my spin became a whirlwind from him cheating, my outlook changed. That's when I decided to creep. I cheated and he cheated… he just didn't know that I was cheating before he went to jail.

Really, he never found out about the other two dudes until the third man, Tomiere, the one I stepped out with and had a baby by, got angry with me and told him in a letter. And, Tomiere only knew of them because I wasn't faithful to his ass. This was typical and predictable behavior from a dude that preyed with conspicuous intentions to get another man's woman. Now that I look back, it was also typical behavior of a woman – me, to cheat on her drug dealer boyfriend when he went to jail. How could he fault me for chasing behind the high of fast money, cars and attention? I wasn't the first woman and damn sure won't be the last to chase behind a luxurious lifestyle. If he hadn't went to jail and left me to get it how I live, I wouldn't have stooped so low to get wit' a nigga in his circle hoping the next man would keep me on top. Shit, women have egos that need to be fed, too!

I opened the glove compartment and got a napkin to wipe the dampness off my face. Then I took the ice cold bottled water and placed it on my forehead to feel the coolness against my skin. I didn't know how much longer I could control my anger.

Kyron and I had only been married for two years. See, there was a period right after he came home from prison when he just didn't want any dealing with me because I had a baby on him. Check this though, like most men, he did have another female that waited patiently for the chance to fuck him again.

Pumpkin was her name. She and Kyron had this on and off again affair. He'd fuck with her during any relationship he was in, including me. The bitch was book smart, but she didn't have street smarts. The wench had the same common sense as the I.Q. of a tree... *none!*

The year that we weren't together, that's when he redirected his attention to his sidepiece and moved in with her. Pumpkin and I have been at war ever since the first time I found out about them back in high school.

Medina and I were attending Kyron and Scabby's high school football game. I was wearing Kyron's varsity football letter jacket and Medina was wearing Scabby's. We made our way to the bleachers to support them by sitting in back of the team. When we got closer, there was Pumpkin with a varsity football jacket on that had Kyron's number on it! Now, I thought you could only get one authentic jacket made, but this fool had two designed. The one I had was his. It was oversized and could wrap around my body at least once. The jacket Pumpkin had on fit her perfectly, which meant to me, it was sized just for her. Jealousy and envy caused me to react the way I did. Medina seen the surging hawk eyes I gave Pumpkin and at the same time, she blocked me from going forth.

"Medina, that bitch got on Kyron's jacket!"

"Oh, lawd." I heard Medina utter. "Maybe it's not his, Serenity. Don't jump to conclusions. Let's just approach the bitch and ask her before we make a scene. 'Cause if it's his, she's straight disrespecting you."

"Hell, fuckin' yeah! She gon' respect me. I don't care how many broads Kyron don' hit off. These ho's gonna respect his #1, plain and simple." I felt Medina grab my arm and try to pull me back. "Get the fuck off of me Medina. If it was Scabby's jacket, you'd already be in that ho's face."

She let go of my arm when I said that. True words: Medina was known to fight a bitch toe to toe over her boo.

"You know you right about that! Let's fuck her up!"

I stepped to Pumpkin, aka Paris Henry, bravely; not even caring about her girls that sat beside her, all looking like fake black Barbie dolls. Pumpkin's long batting eyelashes were about to be yanked off her big bubble face.

"Why you wearing my man's jacket?"

Her energy was unparallel to mine. "Excuse me; I'm trying to watch him play."

Her three little dainty friends emerged in laughter. I turned to face Medina; she had her lips puckered.

"Since the bitch wanna be smart about it, take it from her. He's your man, that's his jacket. Take that shit!"

My lips puckered even further than Medina's as I nodded in agreement. I turned back to Pumpkin and gripped her by the neck and wrestled her to the ground to get what belonged to me.

Needless to say, even though I got the jacket, that wasn't the last encounter, I'd have with her. It's always that one ho with hopes and dreams that she can finally be the main squeeze. Well, Pumpkin was Kyron's. No matter how many times I threatened or confronted her, she'd always find a way to hold onto her wishes of being with him. She didn't mind playing second. Hell, third for all I know. That ho wanted to live the Hustle Bunny life, but she didn't know how to play it, like I did.

To make a long story short, as I said, Kyron and I had our differences right after he came home and he was still pretty much hurt that I stepped out on him. On the other hand, a year went by and neither one of us could stand not being together (well, I influenced that) so he left Pumpkin and we got back together.

Pain is a sure indication that you're going through birth. I believe the pain that we endured when we weren't together was taking us through a new phase of life and since both of us promised to forgive one another and move forward in our relationship, we took it to the next level. Six months in, after we were apart for one year, we got married at the Justice of Peace. We tied the knot on February 14, caught up in the love of Valentine's Day, knowing we weren't ready for this type of commitment. However, it's also been proven that violence simmers below. And, it was the unfaithfulness that neither one of us could ignore that caused havoc in our reunion.

Still, here I was two years later, still married to his sorry ass. I didn't fully forgive him, nor was I fully persuaded that he was faithful to me, but I was determined that Pumpkin wasn't gonna win him. It became my obsession. I'd become so skeptical of him that I began snooping to find out if he was being unfaithful. I kept trying 4-digit numbers on his cell phone voicemail until I finally had the correct password.

Seek and ye shall find.

Well, what I found out is what pushed my temperature over the boiling point. Pandora's box had been opened.

How it Begun

My mother, Ella, just upped and left my father, her estranged husband, because he loved to beat her ass. My mom was scared to contact the police fearing what my Pop might do, so she ran. For a while we relocated to several states, running from him until my mother became tired. Or, I guess daddy got tired of chasing us as well because the last time we moved, we ended up staying for fourteen years. Well, that's what I thought before I found out that my Pop was in the bing for murder... the murder of my mom's side joint. When I asked her about it, she claimed, "Serenity, I was beside myself. I'd lived under the strict rules of your father for so long, I needed a change." Change, meaning a new man. When my Pop found out that Ella was fucking around on him, he damn near killed her. But he was successful at killing her new man. Nevertheless, I haven't had contact with him since I was a youngin' and didn't have plans on it as an adult.

Ella usually stays to herself most times, except for when she goes to church. My dad beat her so much that eventually he broke her spirit. But her grandbabies are her world now, because they love their "mom-mom" unconditionally.

We didn't become stable until we landed in Rosegate, a quiet, but ghetto-ass neighborhood lined up corner to corner with bi-level townhouses in New Castle, Delaware. It was a perfect atmosphere for us. This is where I met Medina, her man, Scabby, "that I call my big brother" and my no-good ass husband, Kyron. That nigga was the love of my life once upon a time. We started out as play boyfriend and girlfriend when I was like eleven years old. We lived three blocks apart and we'd play fight with each other, play hide and go get it, spin the bottle – all the games kids played when we were coming up.

When I started developing, Kyron was the first boy to tell me I had a 'phat' ass. That one compliment sent my young ass on a rollercoaster ride. Although, both of us flirted continuously with each other growing up, I didn't claim him as my boyfriend until I turned thirteen. Whenever new people moved in our neighborhood, we made it known that we were involved, marking our territory. I knew when I was younger that there was a possibility that he was gonna be the man I married. I fantasized about it often as a young girl. My baby had my heart.

Kyron was straight in our puppy stages of love. He taught me so many things about me, and how to push forward to succeed in life. That's the way he was. Then, as risky as it was to sell marijuana and cocaine in Rosegate, back then, Kyron's conscience didn't bother him. He got down for his and he did it with cocky confidence.

Ma'fuckas respected him as a young buck coming of age. His family depended on his street credibility to get extra shit they normally wouldn't get because of the lack of funds. Everybody in the house benefited off of him selling drugs. His family was crazy too. Especially, his cousin JaQuill.

I remember sneaking into his house after school trying to get a quick one in. Living in his Aunt's three bedroom townhouse with damn near his whole family – his mom, his aunt, his two uncles and their sons – it was busy as a 3-ring circus. Sometimes, I hated going over there. Everybody in the family wanted to get up in my business. It was never a time when we sexed without getting caught and it was usually by one of his cousins. They were trying to do the same thing Kyron was – run up in something. So, they'd buss in the room hoping it was free, but catch us in the mix. Then, they'd bribe Kyron out of money to keep it quiet.

"Hurry up, Serenity, before somebody comes home." Kyron always had me rushing to give him some. "Just pull one pant-leg down in case we hear 'em. That way you can get your pants up quicker." He knew how I liked to strip butt ass naked because it was uncomfortable to be fucking with half my clothes on. For him, he was too eager to bust a nut, if he had to stick it through my zipper to get it, he would. "Come on girl, you see this?" He was horny as hell showing me his hard on. I did as he requested and freed up one of my legs from my jeans and lay back on the bottom bunk. I could tell I was in for another rabbit ride the way he was rushing to get inside of me.

"That's not it, Kyron. You're getting too close to my butt hole."

"Put it in then," he responded, impatiently.

I slid my hand down to his stubby penis and swirled it around the mouth of my bottom lips to get it wet some. This drove him crazy. He was pumping hard trying to put it in even with my assistance. Finally, I allowed him to enter me. He damn near smashed my hand between us trying to long stroke it. In which, I wish he hadn't because every time he tried to long stroke it he slipped out of me. He just wasn't built like that. Now, he was thick. True to life, the head of his penis was swollen like a small plump plum and when it got inside of me, it filled the canal up, but long stroking – uh huh, it didn't work.

"Don't be so rough, Kyron." I tensed up gripping deeper into the shaft of his broad back. This made him grind even harder and faster, pounding me with pain. "That hurts, baby." I murmured turning him on I could tell from him humming through his teeth. With one leg in the air dangling over his shoulder and the other laying limp, Kyron pushed himself further inside of me and abruptly stopped.

"Turn over. Let me hit it doggystyle." His strong back was bringing it. I lifted my ass up high so he could scoot underneath me since he was much taller than I was. With one quick stroke, he was back inside me pounding away. This time I was moaning loudly. Backshots always made me act out like that. Kyron started smacking my ass and I imagined it jiggling after each slap. It must've been, because after the third hit – he was releasing what he worked so hard to get – a nut. Soon as he screamed, *"Aaagh,"* one of his cousins flew in the room. My ass was still up high in the air and JaQuill put it out there. "Damn cousin, you tearing 'dat pussy up! Serenity's phat ta' def! You should let me hit that too."

"Yo, shut the door!" Kyron yelled back at him. I was embarrassed once again since this happened on more than one occasion. "Hurry up and pull your pants up," he told me when he was finished. I wanted to at least wash myself up, but he didn't care if I was drippy and whatnot. His job was done and I had to get up outta that room.

"Dang! Can I get a washcloth to clean up?" I asked, holding onto my pants while the semen ran down my leg.

"Wash up at home." He shot back, sending me home with a sticky ass. That was the nastiest feeling after sex and he made me upset anytime he made me leave like that.

Usually after a session, he would walk me home and then leave me to go play football or to hustle. I would go home geeked reporting to Medina minute-by-minute what we did. Kyron wasn't my first, but he was a close runner-up. Sex then was just what it was, sex. No orgasms, mostly penetration and foreplay – kissing, touching, and finger-fucking.

Kyron pretty much had me strapped around his waist during this time. I was so faithful to him it didn't make sense when he was out there dogging me.

When he said jump, I skipped, ran and then asked, how high? I couldn't wear provocative clothing, none of that. I couldn't have friends that he didn't approve of. I couldn't look another man in the face or better yet, even in his direction. If I did, I would get the taste slapped out of my mouth. I didn't understand back then that these were all the signs of a jealous, possessive, insecure man.

I was trapped inside of his world, sometimes feeling like I was in jail. Instead, my C.O. was my man. I made moves according to his rules and regulations. Shoot! That shit got tired after awhile, but to avoid an ass kicking, I still went along with it.

He had power and not just power over me. Kyron was the man even as a young buck. All the dudes in Rosegate looked to him for direction.

At one point in his life he was the star cornerback in high school. He even went to college for three semesters; stayed on campus too. His football career was well on its way to the next level and all of us were supportive of his NFL dreams. However, during one practice his second year, he got injured causing him to miss an entire season. Soon after that, I became pregnant with my first child, Dalya. Things started going downhill for him and instead of sticking and staying, he dropped out of college. There went his NFL dreams and the ma'fuckin money! Too embarrassed to let his family know he was the one who damaged his chances of an NFL career, Kyron put all the blame on me getting pregnant as the reason he came home.

With him back home, with me expecting, it solidified our relationship. Those other hoodrats somewhat faded until he put himself out there again. Money breeds a woman: that is a known fact and the flocks did come. They didn't care that he lived with Ella and me now. I went along with it because I was getting majority of his cash. What I didn't know didn't hurt me.

Kyron hadn't even considered getting us a place of our own and he was making some visible money hugging the block. I pleaded with him to get us a place when Dalya was born, but his version of getting a place was upgrading my mom's house to our comfortability – oversized furniture and king size bedroom sets. And, just like a pure bred negro, instead of getting us a place first, he purchased a car, an Acura Legend. When he got tired of flossing in that, he went big - boy style and purchased a Benz 300 E. Then, he later traded that in for an Excursion. We were getting respect from everybody. He was a young nigga on the grind, flexing past all the old heads in Rosegate still trying to keep a few dollars in their pockets to feed their families. That's when the envy began from both bitches and niggas.

Ella was graceful enough to not make a big fuss about us shacking up, even though she was in church. She felt that because we were young parents, we needed her guidance raising Dalya. Also, she wanted us to do right by each other for the baby's sake. Neither of us had jobs, but what we did have was a baby to take care of and love for each other to hold us together.

Kyron's family wasn't too flattered that he moved out. To them, that meant less money coming in their crib.

In addition to hustling, Kyron had been receiving calls from scouts to try out for the semi-pro football league. The league that accepted the NFL rejects and old injured players looking for another opportunity to get back. After his third tryout with the Diamond Backs, he was put on the roster. He didn't make as much as they did in the NFL playing football, but $2,000 per game was good. The downside of that, it was only a fourteen game season. When the season was over, we solely relied on his trap funds. At the time, for his own selfish reasons, Kyron didn't want me to work. We lived off of my mother anyway, and didn't have to pay one damn bill. She didn't stress us at all; too busy going crazy about Dalya, her first grandbaby. Kyron and I were happy about that. We came and went as we pleased. Which meant, we hit the streets every weekend and sometimes during the week, depending if we were up to it.

After two years of living with her, we finally got a place of our own. It felt good to move out of my mom's house when Dalya turned two. Kyron and I were so excited that we were finally getting our own place. We were quite the ideal couple; other than Pumpkin lingering in limbo. I knew there were others, but Kyron really kept them on the low low. The day we rented our three-bedroom townhouse, we christened every room. Now, I could scream as loud as I wanted when I experienced an orgasm. It took me some time to get one because my man was selfish – used to humping and busting without me getting off mine. The first time I came we were living with my mom. I had to muffle my sounds because my mom's room was right next to mine. Can you imagine experiencing your first orgasm and not being able to moan as loud as you want? Now, I could yell, scream and moan and Kyron could knock the fuckin' headboard against the wall whenever he wanted to without hearing a knock back at us to keep it down. So, you know we were ecstatic when we moved in our own place. The rent was $1,000; peanuts compared to the $10,000 my man was bringing in for the week. It was all-gravy then. We had a good run until Kyron got knocked.

Hard Times

The day Kyron stepped inside of Smyrna prison to do his 3-year bid revealed the destiny of our relationship. The snow is supposed to put the city at peace, but on that blistery winter day, serenity couldn't even calm the storm. We knew (on December 18th to be exact) he had to serve his time. He had been pre-sentenced and pleaded to the judge to allow him some time to handle his affairs for his family before his bid began. Why in the world we'd think (even though we knew) his admitting day would be easy, I'm not sure. It had to be the most suffocating experience for both of us. If he had been arrested unexpectedly and not bailed out, it may have been easier to deal with. Knowing the date only made us face the inevitable.

We hugged, kissed and kissed and hugged some more before he clamped in. The 30 days he was granted to handle his affairs; we made love everyday trying to make a baby. Kyron believed that I could do the time better if I were pregnant. Really, that would make at least nine months go by and I would only have twenty-seven months to stretch. Give or take two months to get my body back up to par. That would leave me with twenty-five months to wait for my man. However, despite our efforts when I was off and even when I was on my period, messy and all, I didn't get pregnant. Medina always ridiculed me for having sex during my "mensy", but with a black or red towel underneath my ass, I could still please my man. I was never ashamed that I partook in this. I did it for my boo. I couldn't cum because it felt too wet, but it never stopped Kyron. His common ass came every time.

The moment they directed Kyron inward behind the metal prison bars, I cried, incapacitating my mind. My perception of reality was with my man. I didn't want to move forward in life without him being in the picture. Coincidentally, Kyron felt the same way from the many letters he sent home the first year he was down. My visits to Smyrna were every Tuesday, faithfully. I had formed a bond with several of the women coming to see their men or family members. It had become routine for us to be greeted by C.O. Bowman with his black – evil – no dick print – having ass. He always had a chip on his shoulder. Trust and believe if your appointment was at 9:30 a.m., you'd better not come at 9:15 a.m., because he'd refuse you entry to the premises. You'd better be to the visiting area before 9:00 a.m., checked in and ready for them to feel you up and scan you with the metal detector to get your visit on.

I always had two visits, both for 45 minutes, but I'd have to wait an additional 45 minutes after the first one to visit Kyron again. Instead of allowing me one visit of an hour and a half, they made me schedule two because they said it was against prison policy. So I had a visit at 9:30 a.m. and then another at 11:30 a.m., going through the same frisking and wanding process twice. I think C.O. Bowman did it just to piss the faithful visitors off because he had a problem with it.

By the second year of this same routine, it wasn't my body, but it was my financial and emotional state that made me slack up with visits. The money Kyron left behind had run out and I did what I could to maintain. I had taken on a job at a Medical Call Center. My job primarily was to call insurance companies to verify that services for patients were paid and paid within the invoiced time frame. I never had to worry about a babysitter, my mom kept Dalya and if she was unavailable, somebody at Kyron's crib was always home.

During Kyron's first stages of his prison term, Medina and I didn't part ways, but we didn't swing like we did when Kyron was home. That changed when I took on the job at M.C.C. Her man, Scabby, was a non-stop hustle 'til he dies type man. If money was on the streets, he had the supply and demand to get that money. He hustled sun up to sun down. It didn't bother him that Medina hung out with me. It freed up his time to do what he needed to do – run his business. Kyron was the opposite of that. He wanted me in the house while he was out doing his "thang". He tried his damnest to keep me away from the circle of dudes that surrounded him. If we seen any of them while we were together, I'd better not fix my mouth to speak. If I spoke to one of them, I knew later when we were alone we'd get into a fight. He was jealous with a capital J, for real.

When Kyron was in prison, Scabby was out on the streets. I became a third leg to Medina and Scabby, tagging along with them to the clubs, restaurants and when they went to malls. We grew close; closer than Kyron wanted. Really, maxing with them is how Tomiere and I came about. We were at the Christiana Mall buying some summer gear. Like most of the hustlers, Scabby stayed shopping in the Foot Locker.

"See, that's why I don't like coming to the mall with females. Y'all take too fuckin' long to get what y'all want." Scabby was ready to go. He'd already purchased what he needed. However, Medina and I were still browsing around. The Foot Locker sales team was bringing out different styles and color of Nike's for both of us.

"Go calm your man, would ya. He's bugging for nothing." I stood up glancing down at the silver and white with black trim sneaks. "These are hittin'. Let me bag these." Out of the corner of my eye, I watched as Scabby exited the store to give a pound to Tomiere, who was with two other dudes that were unfamiliar to me.

"Give me some of that good money, nigga! I heard you creamin' 'em out there." I heard Tomiere say to Scabby.

The chills that used to anger my bones were now sending warmth through them for this snitch – ass nigga, Tomiere. He knew damn well he shouldn't have taken the stand to testify against

Kyron. Yeah, he was with Kyron when he got busted. His excuse to Kyron was, "Man, they had a bench warrant for my ass if I didn't appear. I didn't need that over my head." Not to be on his side, but it wasn't his testimony that actually sent Kyron to jail. It was the three ounces of cocaine that landed him the mandatory 3-year sentence. But still, Tomiere didn't have to go out like that. Kyron hated him ever since, saying that he was a sucker type snitch ass dude. Well, he damn sure didn't look like a sucker type cat in his beige camouflage Sixers fitted with his brown and beige army fatigues on. That brother was sharp and showing out with his hanging platinum chains. Not to mention his diamond stud that protruded from his ear. He had me stuck on him for a moment until Medina yanked on my skirt.

"Ain't that Tomiere?" She was trying on a pair of Nike Shox and a pair of Timbs with high rubber heels.

"Yeah, that's that snitch ma'fucka," I acknowledged, with my eyes still on him and Scabby.

"Damn that nigga look tasty even as a snitch, right?" I was glad that Medina seen the same thing I did in him. Snitch was the furthest thing from my mind right then, but the word came out so easy to show that I was still loyal to my man.

"He sure the fuck do! All 200 pounds of that blacktino," I quickly admitted to her. My eyes eagerly waited for his Black and Latino ethnic mix to glance my way. "Over the years that boy filled out – got milk?" I laughed. The way his clothes fell on his body made me believe he had a strong game. Maybe it wasn't the case, but I believed it at the time. His swagger was nice – real thorough.

"Bitch, I knew you would play yourself like that. That's why I asked. I was just testing you," she hit me on the leg. "He's always been real flamboyant to me."

"Why you say that?" I knew what she meant. Whenever Tomiere spoke, he was loud and wanted to be heard by all.

"'Cause ho, no matter how good the nigga look, he still turned on ya man."

"Understood, but it's not like I'm try'na holla at him."

"Serenity, who the fuck do you think you're talking to? *Huh?* We've been friends since the 6th grade. Sometimes, I know you better than you know yourself. I see that look in your eyes. It's the same look that you had for Lewis and Dabee... you *wanna* fuck Tomiere."

She had to bring up Lewis and Dabee, two dudes I crept with when Kyron was home. Every time she called herself getting angry with me, she'd bring that up like she was a national spokesperson for Kyron. That was one reason I didn't like messing with Medina sometimes, she always thought she knew my next move. I didn't even want to play her down, but she was correct. Fucking him wasn't exactly on the top of my agenda. First, I wanted to get to know him a little better than I had.

"If I said yes, then what?"

"Then, I'd say you a grimey bitch, that's what. But, do you! I knew you wouldn't be able to hold it down for my boy. You ain't the soldierette that you confess to be."

"Fuck you Medina!" I blurted, getting a little uptight on my way to pay for my shit causing shoppers to stare our way.

She laughed it off. "Nah, fuck him, not me. I'm not into women."

Looking through the window display, I caught Tomiere casually eying me. Medina and I paid for our new jump-off's (sneaks) and met up with the fellas outside of the store in the crosswalk of the mall. This was an unlikely time and I couldn't understand the impact that Tomiere had on me as we approached.

"How you doin', Tomiere?" I said when we walked up like I had been chattin' with him all along. Before the court case, I never said a word to him around Kyron. Not that I didn't want to, I found him sexy as hell, but Kyron wouldn't allow me to talk to any of them. Just for this reason, I guess. You can't keep a cat locked down forever; they will always find a way to get free. And, that's how I felt, free! Besides, Tomiere and I did share a historical moment together before Kyron and I became a couple.

"It's all love, pretty lady," he concluded with his eyes scanning over me.

Scabby raised up his arms in a U-shape like a football goal on the sides of his head like, "What the fuck?" Kyron and Scabby were cool, but he wasn't in Scabby's main circle. Medina shook her head and her and Scabby stepped off. I stood there waiting for more chitchat as Tomiere's boys stepped inside the Foot Locker.

"Serenity, we're headed to Baker's to check out the new shit, you comin'?" Medina asked, nodding her head in her direction as to tell me to come on before I got myself into trouble.

"I'll meet y'all there," I responded, with my eyes still on Tomiere. When they left out of earshot, I said to him, "You could at least send Kyron a few stacks, you know. Since you still getting' it."

Tomiere was very quick with it.

"Listen man, I don't owe ya man shit. He knows the rules and the consequences of the game. They caught him dirty. I ain't have shit to do with that. It wasn't nothing I could say or do to change that."

In Kyron's defense, I called myself drilling him, knowing that really I wanted him to make an advance on me so I could get his number. But I didn't want it to be that obvious. He would never be able to say that I came on to him first if, and when, Kyron found out.

"Yeah, but did you have to take the stand against him? I thought Kyron was your manz."

"C'mon man, you talking jibberish. Did he really think that I would get on the stand to say that he just purchased the coke from me? What hustla you know gon' do that? Let me answer that for you – none!"

I felt him on that and didn't know what else to say. That was the only topic I had to spark up conversation with him. I imagined I should've asked him how he got away scott-free and they found the drugs in his car, but on Kyron. Then, I really didn't need to ask. He'd already proven that he testified on the prosecutor's behalf.

"Well, you could still look out for him. Y'all were getting money together."

"Correction, I was supplying and he was buying for his clientele."

"Same difference; money was being exchanged. Anyway, I need to catch up to my people. I'll get back." If he wasn't interested, I knew I'd walk off empty handed. If he was, I wouldn't.

Instead of letting me step away, he reached out to me. That's when I knew he was game.

"Hold up, pretty lady. You're right, I could send your man a stack or two," he conceded, peeling off two hundreds from his money wad.

"That's it?" I frowned, letting the greed of the money get to me while I was playing his paper carefully.

"Nah, there's more where it came from," he said slyly trying to enhance me with his dollars. He didn't know I had already bit and swallowed the bait. "Here, plug my number in your cell. Whenever you need cake... for your man," he hesitated, stressing *for your man*, "Hit me up and I'll take care of that, cool?"

I pulled out my light grey Boost Mobile to save his number without a thought.

"Damn, shorty... you got a *Boost?* Pretty as you are wit' a Boost Mobile. Don't worry, I'ma strap you. Here, take another $500 and invest in a real phone. Get ya'self a Chocolate or a Razor phone. If your credit is an issue, they even have an easy pay plan without committing yourself to a contract. You need to handle that ASAP!"

I was hoping he didn't have X-ray vision inside my heart because my thoughts contaminated my feelings. I wanted to get wit' him. The shopping music coming out of the mall stereo system suddenly became soothing. People walking by laughing and conversing became loud overshadowing the soothing sounds that were ringing in my ears. I knew if he'd drop that amount and I only talked slick, when I gave him some of this good stuff, I'd get G's. Hopefully, I couldn't be easily read because the $700 that he just dropped in my hands had me ready to buss out in a happy dance. *Heeyy!*

"Yeah, that's cool," I replied saving his number temporarily until I purchased a new phone. Now, I was in a hurry to meet back up with Scabby and Medina feeling like I'd just scored big, when $700 was really chump change compared to the money that Kyron used to hit me off with.

"*I'm a bonfide hustla,*" Tomiere began to sing as I trailed away with the notion that he threw that out there for me to catch it.

I thought about our "historic" moment walking in the opposite direction of him. Tomiere was more than just a snitch that took my man down. He was the young man that split my golden "V" into two, making me a woman. Right before I officially claimed Kyron as my boyfriend, Tomiere had spent the night over his friend's house in "the gate". It was a lot of us outside that day playing around on the basketball courts. Kyron and all his boys were out there too. It was nearing dust and many of them had a curfew, including me. Kyron called himself leaving with his boys, leaving me behind. The other girls out there had partnered up with their little boyfriends trying to get a few hugs and kisses before they had to go in. Suave and manipulating before his time,

Tomiere stayed back and told me he'd walk me home. I was fine with that because I liked Tomiere. He was definitely the runner up to Kyron. Instead of going straight there, we pit stopped behind the church a few blocks away from the court. The church had steps that led down into the back entrance door of the basement. We gently took each step until we were out of view. I didn't know what I was about to get into, but Tomiere did. He began kissing and rubbing me all over my small perky breast making them erect. The feeling was strange, but it felt good and I hadn't stopped him. I had on my basketball shorts with the expandable waist that were easy access to get down. Tomiere never said anything; both of us remained silent. I hadn't truly realized that I was about to let him take my virginity until I felt the force of his penis ripping and splitting through my protective vaginal shield. In a matter of ten minutes, it was over just like that – my innocence was gone. The way he took charge this wasn't his first time. Tomiere kissed me on my lips when he was done and told me to hurry up so we could catch up with everybody else. He never told anybody to my knowledge about that day. I guess he got what he wanted.

How embarrassing would it have been to tell someone at that young age, I lost my virginity outside in the back entrance of a Pentecostal church that my mother was a member of? After that, Tomiere and I never hooked up nor did we talk about what happened that day. He didn't even say anything when Kyron reported to everyone that I was his girl and I was off limits to other boys. I never even told Medina that Tomiere was the guy that hit this first. I led her to believe that Kyron was my first. I guess you could say I was too ashamed to tell her about the experience and how young I was when I lost my virginity. I don't know why I lied, but I did.

I scurried through the mall to find my ride hoping that they didn't decide to leave me. If they did, I'd have to ask Tomiere for a ride. And, as twitchy as I felt, I may have let him hit that night. I peeped in several stores since they weren't inside of Baker's like Medina said they would be.

"It's about time, whore. We've been to three different stores since we left you," Medina acknowledged, coming out of Victoria Secrets with three big bags.

"Hot damn, somebody's about to get their freak on," I teased.

"Stop trying to throw me for a loop. What could you possibly be talking to him about this damn long?"

"Let it go, Medina. I'm a grown ass woman."

She was starting to bother me. Whether she was trying to look out for my best interest or not, I didn't feel like her drilling me. She began to sound like Kyron when he was giving me the third degree.

"You are not my man, okay!"

"You better be glad, because if I was, you'd be fucked up by now," she bucked her bright eyes letting up on me as we approached the food court.

Scabby acted like he didn't want to look my way when we sat down to eat, so I jump-started the conversation between us.

"What's wrong wit' you? You feeling stressed up in your chest, what?" I asked after placing my Chinese food platter down beside him. Medina was at the Pizzeria counter getting them a few slices of pizza.

"Kyron and me ain't really like that, but you know that ain't right," he stated bass-less, and I took it for what it was worth.

"Not you, too. Damn! I ain't do nuthin' wrong." Here I was explaining myself for the second time.

"Fuck it! If you wanna get that niggas money go 'head. I don't know shit. My name is Bennett and I ain't in it," he passively joked about it.

"That's why I love you, nigga." I smiled at him scuffing up his half braided, half wild Afro head. He always co-signed my wrong doings.

"Kyron's gonna kill your ass. Keep fucking around, seriously," he switched back up on me. "You 'dat man's Queen, do what you gotta do, but don't play yourself out here like most ho's when their man goes to jail. I mean you can play a little, but keep it on the low. Don't embarrass the man by taking it public. That's all I'm saying. Because if he finds out, he's gonna go after you and the man you're fucking around on him with. I know that much about him."

Now, this much I knew from my mom's experience, but I didn't believe it would happen to me. Kyron wasn't a killer even if you pushed him.

"How many times do I have to tell you, I ain't do nuthin'? I've been holding it down for him."

"Yo, you don't have to explain it to me. You can get money from Tomiere, but at the price of what? You ready to deal with his shit? Because it comes with a price," he stressed. "Yeah, and I've been noticing since you got that job, you've changed. They say don't give a woman independence. Once y'all get a taste of that, y'all are never the same."

"Knock it off. If I didn't work, I'd still be borrowing money from you and Medina."

Medina came back from getting their food and sat down opposite of Scabby removing his three slices from the serving tray.

"What y'all talking about?" she hinted like we were keeping secrets from her.

"You, and when you're finally going to give this knucklehead a baby," I implied and both of us waited for her to respond.

"*Shiiit*, not me. I don't want any kids. I love my life too much. I'm having too much fun to mess that up by taking on a responsibility. Besides, I don't have it like you. My mom ain't watching nobody's kids. Not even on holidays down her house in Maryland."

"So you're saying you don't ever want to have kids?" Scabby pressed. He had expressed that he wanted a son or two, to me before. I'm sure he mentioned the same to his woman.

"No, baby. I wasn't saying that. Just not at this time. It doesn't mean we can't keep practicing," she declared leaning over the table to kiss him.

I somewhat envied the relationship that they shared. Both of them were carefree. They didn't put strings on the relationship like Kyron did. I only knew of one guy Medina jumped off with and that was with the guy that broke her virginity and she sincerely regrets doing that. When Scabby found out, he left her ass for four months. She went through it and who do you think help mend the wound... me baby, that's who. Both of them were suffering and I couldn't take listening to her crying and him being stubborn about it. Nah, but truly, I think Scabby was fronting the whole time. He just wanted space to hit some strange and say he did it when they were broken up. It wasn't like he never cheated on her; he did many times before.

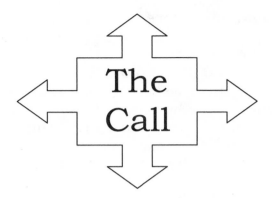

The Call

"Yo, why don't you ride through and scoop me up?" Tomiere suggested, with his way of greeting me on the phone. He hustled in Simmons Garden, another hood community that was 'bout it. That was only fifteen minutes walking distance from where I lived. I knew I had no business picking him up in the truck that Kyron had been paying for, but I needed the money to keep the car note up if he wanted to still have it when he came home.

"Scoop you up for what? Where's your car?" He didn't need to know that I was game and pressed for his dividends. So, I played somewhat resistant.

"It's getting detailed at my shop. You coming through or what? I don't have time for procrastinators. I got business to take care of." Here this man was taking control of our conversation. Why I felt indebted to him... the ma'fuckas cash, that's why. The money kept pulling me in.

"I'm coming through in 'bout, uh, ten minutes. Be ready, too. I don't need people whispering about us." Especially since Kyron's cousin JaQuill was always out and about.

"If you scared, don't come then," he banged the phone on me. I was baffled for a second. This dude was playing me like I was a bird and I wasn't that topnotch breed that Kyron bred. He was treating me like secondhand clothing. I should've bucked up to him and said, "Fuck you, you snitch," but instead it became more of a turn on. A challenge even, to toy with him.

I was a size twelve after I gave birth to Dalya and my stomach had gone back flat. So when I put on my low-rise Apple Bottom capris my ass fit lovely in them. I had on a lavender camisole top that matched the lavender trim around the pocket of my capris. My silver accessories went perfect, as did my open toe stilettos exposing my pretty pedicured toes that were painted a lavish lavender and silver.

When I pulled over to the detail shop on New Castle Avenue it was packed with people washing cars or standing around just kickin' it. It was enough of them out there for me to quickly make a U-turn so I wouldn't be seen with him, but I didn't. Failing to adhere to the advice that Scabby gave to me, I fed into Tomiere's egotistical state and whipped the Excursion right on the side of him getting myself into trouble. It's funny how we don't think about the consequences when we're in the midst and that... I was. All of the dudes surrounding Tomiere knew Kyron, and I suspected that from the shocked expressions on their faces, at the first opportunity they were

47

gonna put it on blast that they seen me approaching Tomiere.

"Get out the truck," Tomiere mandated sticking his head inside the driver's side window. The weather was fair and there was a steady breeze making Tomiere's open striped button-up flap outwardly. His eyes were glistening and the white around his pupils appeared bleached, compared to the bloodshot red eyes of the guys standing behind him smoking a blunt. I eyed the scene intensely hoping that none of Kyron's family was out there; especially, JaQuill. His ignorant ass would've made a major scene. Still, it was enough people out there for my "little visit" to get back to Kyron.

"You playin', you see how ya boys looking at me now."

"Fuck 'em! You came for me didn't you?" He backed up from the Excursion and said again, "Get out the car, Serenity." He was truly testing how far I'd go for him. I should've said no to the games he was playing, but when he pulled out his fat stack and counted it in front of me, he knew that my motivation for cash would make me get out.

I slowly stepped down grabbing onto the side bar to ease down on my stilettos.

"Come here with ya pretty ass." He was slouched a bit still counting his money. His boys attentively watched any move I made. "What kind of phone did you buy?"

I retrieved my new Nextel 930 to show him that I didn't need the easy pay plan from Verizon.

"Yeah, that's more of ya speed. I hope you tossed that cheap ass Boost that ya man got you out here on the strength with." That was definitely a power punch that he threw to let the others know that Kyron left me empty handed – broke, busted and disgusted.

In defense of all my people that had to get a Boost Mobile I stated, "Ain't nothin' wrong with having a Boost if that's all you can afford. Besides with this new phone, I had to sign that two-year contract you were talking about. I don't have to worry about that though, since you got the bill."

"Mmm hmm, I got it as long as I got you," he slickly slid that in, and then handed me $400 like he was "that nigga".

I was standing there out in the open of his detail shop where all the hustler's frequented, playing *mind games* with this fool, about to become his new hustle bunny to get cash from him. Cars were steady pulling up watching us as money left his hand in exchange for mine. This had to be his plan for us to be out in plain view for the hood to see.

"I thought we were leaving?"

"My ride will be done in less than ten minutes, why should I leave now? You can't chill with me until it's finished?"

"Well, I do have things to do."

"Like what? Kyron had 'dat ass on lockdown. I'm sure you love this free time."

Sure I loved my free time. It was a breath of fresh air doing whatever and whomever I wanted without Kyron breathing down my back.

"I do have a job and a daughter at home, Tomiere."

"I guess you don't work on Saturdays, 'cause if you did, you'd be there. What you wanna do, go get your daughter and take her shopping? I know her daddy can't provide for her, so I'll step up."

While it was kind of him to help out, Kyron was a damn good father to his baby girl. She never went without and wanted for nothing. Yet, I kept letting Tomiere make it seem like Kyron was tight when it came to us.

"Why don't you do this, call me when you're ready." I dropped one ass cheek after the other going back to the Excursion. His openness to dis Kyron in front of his boys made me upset.

"Naah, better yet, take another $400 and take ya shorty out shopping. When you're done hit me and I'll take you out to show you how special you are. You know I've always wanted to get back with that." This told me that all along he was waiting for a spot, letting all those around him know at one point we had a connection. The attraction had always been there since we were pre-teens.

My lip-gloss was poppin' as I began to smile my way back to get the additional funds from him. "Thank you. I'll hit you later. And, hopefully this time you'll be alone. I don't do well with crowds of people."

I got back inside the truck and pulled off watching him in the rearview mirror. I could see him cleverly smile as I faded down the Avenue.

I called Medina to see if she wanted to go to the mall with me. Besides, I needed to share with her what I was doing.

"Medina, you busy?"

"Not really. I just got finished cowboy riding Scabby, but I'm free now. What's up?" Her voice was in a hurried exhausted tone. She literally must have just hopped off of her man.

"Ride to the mall with me."

"I thought money was tight. You got gas money, a new cell and money for the mall. Girl, you doin' it! Or, doing him, one."

She knew me.

"Well, not exactly. I'm trying to get caught up on my bills. You know I was behind in rent, so all of my money was going towards that to stop the eviction process. Plus, you know I was behind on my high ass Delmarva Power electric bill."

Medina paused, "Then why are we going to the mall?"

"I'll tell you when I get there. You're riding, right?"

"Sure, why not."

As I neared Medina's house, I saw Scabby getting into his wine colored Lumina with the dark limousine tint that was only two shades lighter than his skin color.

"Scabby!!" I hollered at him.

"What's up anrie? I heard you were at Tomiere's joint giving niggas something to talk about. Niggas will let information leak back to Kyron to show him that he has a flaw in his diamond. Pay attention to what you're doing."

"I will. Just know that I'm still a precious gem." That's how quickly the news spread. I grinned when he called me "anrie". Sometimes I could be very levelheaded but there were other times when the anrie side of me prevailed. Those were times I was about to do something I didn't have any business doing.

Medina came trotting down the steps with a waxed fishscale hairdo from one of the Baltimore salons.

"That's cute. How come you didn't ask me if I wanted a Baltimorean hair do? You know I love how they get down."

"You were at work when I went yesterday. Anyway, Scabby had some business to handle down there and while he was doing it, I took it upon myself to get my hair did."

"Okay, let's go. I need your honest opinion."

"Uh oh, what have you done now? I knew it, you sexed him didn't you?"

I grinned at her.

"Please buckle your seatbelt before we take this ride." From the corner of my eye I could see her staring at me. Most times she was never judgmental and I could pretty much tell her everything. Now, she'd throw a few things up in my face every so often, but not that much.

"Tomiere keeps giving me money."

I whipped through the traffic to get us to the Concord Mall on Route 202, waiting for her response. We'd passed two traffic lights and she still hadn't said a thing.

"Well?"

"Well Serenity, what do you want me to say? The nigga is only putting a deposit down on you, as he should. Ain't nothing for free. He'll keep throwing money your way as long as you give him something in return."

"Is that right? So, all I have to do is keep talking and he'll keep passing off? I'ma be a talking ma'fucka then." I was playing clueless with her. I knew he wanted to get in my panties; I just wanted her take on it. "... 'Cause that's all I'm doing is talking."

"Yeah, for now. I can't take anything away from him. Tomiere is all that. He's fine as hell with his fine blacktino ass. He's got a lot going on for him, and not just hustling. He has legit businesses and making good money from them. I heard the nigga dick is fat like his pockets, which means he's got the full package."

"Got-damn, is it? Who told you that? I gotta watch you. Let me find out you hit him off and that's why you don't want me fuckin' with him."

I couldn't remember anything about the size of his penis. I only remembered it stung when he broke me in.

"Please... Scabby is 10½ and fatter than a jumbo sausage over cooked."

I immediately felt my bottom lips twitch when she said that. Every woman I knew wanted a man with size (major size) that could put it down in the bed. I know I was like family, but she shouldn't have told me how fat Scabby and Tomiere's dick were as horny as I was. It had been one year plus, some more days, and I hadn't even touched a dick. I would never overstep my boundaries though (...?); Scabby and Medina were true to me.

"Anyway, so what do you think?"

"I think you're about to sink without a life jacket on. Are you willing to lose Kyron over him? You know how boastful both of them are. When Kyron finds out... and he will, he's gonna stop fucking with you."

"He's in jail. I'm the one holding it down for us. Tomiere's been helping me pay my debts and keeping me laced with extra money. He even gave me duckets to take Dalya on a shopping spree."

"Stop making excuses, Serenity. Dalya don't need or want for nothing. Besides that, she's living with Ella and Kyron's family looks out for her as well. Girl, you got it made. So, how hard is it for you to catch up on your bills? You've been on your job for three months and if it's that bad take on a second job. I know you're getting caught up by now. You weren't that behind in your bills unless you've been spending recklessly."

I made an easy left turn into the Concord Mall parking lot and parked in the Sear's area.

"You may be somewhat correct. I am finally starting to get caught up, but damn if it don't feel good to have a man treat me. I haven't felt this special since Kyron was home. It feels *hella* good to spend somebody else's money. I deserve to be treated special."

Medina exited out of the truck and walked side by side with me as we entered the lower entrance of the mall.

"I can see if Kyron didn't spend on you, but he did. All the money that came in the house was for you and Dalya. He hustled his ass off for you when he could've left you when he went to college. Instead, he couldn't stay away from your funky ass and came home."

Boy, did she really have a misconception.

"He didn't come back for me. He came back because of his injury that knocked him outta the season. *That's* why his ass came back."

"Serenity, you were pregnant with his baby! That's why he dropped out. He wanted to be there for his boo. He did more than miss a season. He missed an opportunity of a lifetime."

"All hussy, shut up! You always throw somethin' up in my damn face! Maybe he did, maybe he didn't. It still doesn't mean he's here for us now."

"Forget it, Serenity. I see you've already made your mind up. Believe me; I know it's hard for you. Hell, it would be hard for me, too. Take it from me," she patted her scalp from it itching, "I jumped off with Larry Love trying to see if the feeling was still there and got busted. I almost lost Scabby forever and you know I can't live without my other rib. I will never jeopardize my relationship with him again. That's why I'm telling you to think, gurl... **hard**, before you do it. Don't make the same mistake I did."

Larry Love was Medina's first love that broke her in as well. Their fling was in no way a comparison to what I was about to encounter. It was Medina who approached Larry when Scabby was in jail to feel his bone. It wasn't about money. *Who was she trying to fool? Why was she try'na compare my situation to hers?* She never loved no man the way she loved Scabby. This meant, she damn sure didn't fuck Larry Love to find out if the love was still there. They were horny teenagers when Larry Love hit it. She'd been with Scabby ever since she and Larry Love parted ways. They were the only two she let get it. Scabby knew this too. Medina was one step next to pure. For him to luck up on a female that only had been hit by one nigga was a gold mine: a jackpot at the end of his rainbow.

"I hear you, but can I tell you this? I've always thought Tomiere was cute. And, he always smells so fresh when I'm around him."

"That's crazy because the only other time you were around him was when he was with your man. So, all those times you were lusting over him?"

Our paces picked up as we walked through the mall to the Kids Foot Locker.

"How about it was all those times he was lusting after me? How 'bout you say that! I'm not the only guilty party here."

Just when we entered the store, Pumpkin was at the register with the two little girls that were her foster sisters. One was Dalya's age and the other was slightly younger than her. They probably were only eleven months apart. That's how close in age they were. I said loud enough for her to hear me, "Lemme see what I'ma buy Dalya. I know her daddy would like to see her in these." I picked up the new pink and white Nike's and a pair of clear and red trimmed Air Force Ones. "What you do think, Medina? You think Kyron would like these on his baby girl?" Childishly, I behaved to get under Pumpkin's skin, who was ignoring me, all dressed up in her Sunday's best.

She worked as an IT Manager for a Pharmaceutical company and was making plenty of money. She was all right in the face and pretty smart, but I never could stand the bitch.

Peacefully, Medina sat down chatting back and forth with me until Pumpkin paid for her merchandise and the three of them left.

"That's crazy. Every time you see that girl, those old feelings come out and you're ready to get at her, which lets me know she's still pushing ya buttons. If you didn't still have love for Kyron, you wouldn't act like this."

I got up and picked out two pair of sneaks and two sweatsuits for Dalya to take to the register.

"Pumpkin's one of those sneaky, underhanded bitches that's why. You bet' not trust her around ya man. She's the type that will do ya man and smile up in your face, like she hadn't. NE-way, I never said I was going to be through with him. I'm just planning to have a little side fling, like he did me. I still have love for my man."

"You'll never let that go, will you?"

"No, and I never will: once a cheater, always a cheater. Why should I be faithful? Have you totally forgiven Scabby for cheating on you?" She could never try to chastise me when she did the same damn thing.

"Yes, I have. I'm the one who chose to stay."

"Yeah, but you're also the one that chose to cheat after he cheated. So, don't run that BS on me. Shit, an affair might be helpful. I need some bad."

"That's why they created adult toys."

"Girl, I need to feel some hot, thick dick up in me. Not no damn mold of a dick. And if what you said is true... Tomiere is just the man to give it to me. Gurl, a good dick and plenty of cash – that's a beautiful thing," I chuckled. "Now let's hit the Children's Place."

I didn't need to get her approval. I already had my answer. I just didn't want to feel that guilty when I did it, so I told her.

Scratch That

"Yo, where you want me to scoop you?"

Tomiere didn't say, "Hi, what's up, Serenity", none of that. He was always direct. He got straight to it. I didn't know whether I should have him pick me up at home or if I should've met him in a discrete location.

"Well, you could've at least said hello."

"Yo, quit playing. You know who this is. It's that nigga to fill ya void."

I laughed softly admiring how arrogant he was. If it was a void that he needed to fill, he had to dig deep.

"Where are we going?" I hadn't completely gotten dressed. In fact, I was lounging on the red leather chaise, rummaging through a few magazines with my black lace panty and bra set on waiting for him to call. His call determined if I was getting dressed or not.

"Bring an overnight bag."

"Overnight? You move fast don't you?"

"Yeah and so do your hands everytime you see money. I'm coming to ya crib, ai'ight."

I swear he said that just to see what I would say. "No, don't come here! Uh ahn, don't do that."

"Don't tell me you're scared. As many times as I've been to ya crib, won't nobody think nothin'."

"Tomiere, everybody knows that you and Kyron got beef. Stop playing. I'll park my car in the back parking lot of the church in front of the Gate. Don't none of them hoodlums, go to church so they won't see us."

Momentarily, the silence nerved me. I took it that he wasn't comfortable with that.

"Listen ma, I ain't a second hand dude playin' from the bench. All this hiding and sneaking, really, I ain't for it. I got women constantly on my machine try'na holla. If you're too ashamed to be seen with me, yo, don't fuck wit' me."

I rose forward from the chaise and planted my bare feet on the black and red Oriental rug.

"Wait a minute, Tomiere. Kyron and I have been together for years. I can't disrespect him like that, you should ---"

"I should what?" he cut in, "Ma, you disrespected the man when you accepted my money. Matter fact, this ain't even 'bout him. This is about you and me. Meet me in back of the church in a half hour."

As troubled as he seemed, he still let me get my way. This time our meeting wouldn't last only ten minutes like it did when we were younger.

I began to say, "Forget it," but he hung up the phone on me. I had dealt with Kyron's possessive ways and I sure wasn't about to deal with his.

I eased up off the chaise and walked my ass upstairs to raid my closet. I wasn't certain what to wear because he never told me where we were going for me to play my gear right. I had three outfits in mind hoochie, hoochie, and hoochie! Kyron hated when I wore tight or revealing clothing. Since, he'd been gone; I wore at least a revealing top to show off my plump cleavage four times a week when the weather was appropriate.

I pulled out a scoop neck black vintage t-shirt with silver letters – PRICELESS – going across the center of my breast. I pulled out my only black pair of House of Dereon jeans and my black leather boots with silver heels. I had the perfect Prada long strap bag to accent it with my white gold accessories. I got real casual cute on him. I didn't want to over do it.

Just when I finished dabbing the new Paris Hilton scent on my inner arms, the house phone rang. When I picked it up, I immediately heard, *"You have a collect call from... Kyron"*. Men have a sixth sense just as well as women and my man had timed me right.

"Hey baby," I said after hitting the number 5 to accept his call. I quietly placed my keys on the marble kitchen counter. I even tried to stop the creaking noise coming from the floor from the weight of my heels.

"Where you been?" I called the house twice earlier." He sounded deeply suspicious. "Where's Dalya?"

I was mesmerized by his introduction. First, it was Tomiere and now it was him. To his own resolve he spat out, "Never mind, I already know. She's at Ella's. Are you going somewhere tonight? I heard that you've been going out with Medina and Scabby lately."

"That's true." He finally let me get a word in. "But I'm not going anywhere tonight. Really, I was just in the bed dozing off watching some television. I'm trying to rest up from the long week I've had. My job is stressful, okay." I squatted carefully trying to fix my pant leg and accidentally hit my keys that went tumbling down on the kitchen floor. *Damn*, I hissed.

"What was that?" he stressed with his bionic listening skills.

"I knocked over my cup, that's all."

"That's funny if you're falling asleep in the bedroom, its carpet on the floor. How come that sounded like a tile or vinyl floor that the cup fell on?"

"What are you accusing me of Kyron?"

"Exactly what I thought, you're lying to me!"

The same tightness that filled my stomach when he was home always accusing me of cheating overcame me. This time this was the jumpstart I needed to turn my engine on full speed.

"I'm tired of you insinuating that I'm lying to you and I'm out here picking up the slack that you left. You're only acting this way because Pumpkin came to see you!" He thought I didn't know that she was the one filling my spot every week since I'd started my job.

"It's my people locking down the visits, Serenity. If you were on the jack, you'd secure the spot first."

When I called the prison to find out who had the visits on lock, they'd never tell me who was scheduled, but I had a female acquaintance from my hood that was visiting her man, too, name Urslynn – "Urs" for short. Every neighborhood has a former dime turned crack addict: ours was Urs.

Once a beautiful thick cinnabon queen, Urs had gone downhill in the last five years. She was a few years older than I was and once a female that everyone admired in the Gate. She had most of the men's attention, maybe too much, and instead of working that in her favor, it backfired on her. For a young person getting high, she still had some respect, even if it was only for those few seconds when she was buying rocks. I looked for her to give me a word or two because she always had the inside scoop on what was poppin' in our hood. She was pretty cool, sometimes too straightforward, but nonetheless, cool. Urs knew Pumpkin and told me that she was the one coming to see my man on the regular.

You have one minute remaining, the operator sounded.

I counted down the sixty seconds and couldn't wait to hang up the phone with him. He thought he was going to play me, but I was about to show him what it felt like to get played.

Never kick a dog when it's down – *why not?* Shit, it's down already, how much lower can it go?

Times were changing for me and so were my feelings.

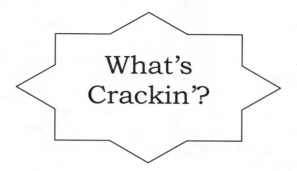

What's Crackin'?

"Yo, you a smut! And, I hope my cousin **never** fucks with you again!" JaQuill embarrassed me in front of Tomiere.

I was ducking Kyron's calls and refused to see him because I was four months pregnant. From JaQuill's expression, he had heard I was expecting. It had only been six months since I began fooling with Tomiere and I fucked around and got knocked up! I won't use the lame excuse, "the condom broke" or "I was on the pill", because this wasn't the case. We were going raw and it felt hella good until I found out a seed had been planted.

With sullen shameful eyes, I batted my lashes twice wanting to get back at JaQuill, but I was wrong. He was hurt that I dissed his cousin and got pregnant by the man that sent him to jail. Who wouldn't be? I understood that.

"You'd best get goin' talkin' that whack shit to my girl." Tomiere stood up for me even though I didn't want him to. JaQuill had a right to be angry. I was apart of his family.

I wanted to stay stuck and livid with myself for being so stupid! I knew for sure that Kyron was through with me. I'd never seen that bitch Pumpkin give me a second or third stare the way she had when she was trying to figure out if what she heard was true. It was like her world opened up when she finally realized I was pregnant. I bet she went full blast at Kyron then. I hated the way anybody associated with Kyron gawked at me when they noticed my belly protruding forward.

"Fuck you, nigga! Serenity you foul! And, if I didn't love my cousin like I do, to see him hurt forever, I'da took you out for straight disrespecting him like that!" JaQuill then held his shirt up exposing' his gat for us to see.

Right next to him was some pitch-black dude and another dude that I didn't recognize, waiting for JaQuill to give them a signal to make a move.

To avoid any further shame, I disappeared to Tomiere's Nissan Titan SE and let them exchange words and hopefully not gunfire.

JaQuill was not the type to back down from anything or anybody and neither was Tomiere, so both egos struggled with who would be the bigger man. Instead of JaQuill leaving, he came over to the passenger's side window and pounded on the glass, harassing me.

"Nobody's gonna be watchin' Dalya so you can ho. So go pick her up. When I get to the house she bet not still be there. Or, the next time I see you, it won't be nice. I don't give a fuck if you're pregnant or not, I'ma lay you down!"

I hadn't even put the window down, but I heard him loud and clear. I just wanted to get away from this crazy ass fool. Tomiere finally got in the truck and rode off leaving JaQuill behind as dust danced off the back of the truck.

"You shoulda never fucked that dude anyway." Tomiere's nostrils were flaring. "We wouldn't have this problem. That nigga gon' make me kill his cousin if he keeps talkin' off track to me. Why'd you make him ya man, anyway? That dude ain't cut like me!"

His comment threw me off a bit. It was foolish that he felt I was all his. My heart was always with Kyron, even though I was with Tomiere now. I was only four months and stressed out like I was in my ninth month of pregnancy.

I'd allowed Tomiere in Kyron's treasure place and he'd struck gold. To him, I was his woman and we were a family now. The child I would bare was his firstborn. This made it even worse. Now, he was overprotective of every damn thing. The things I ate. What liquids I drank. He even made sure I properly exercised and was taking the prenatal vitamins that I was prescribed. I mean going overboard with it. Every week we were shopping for the baby. I tried to explain to him it was bad luck, but he didn't believe that.

I felt Tomiere casting his eyes on me as I sat complacent.

"You heard me didn't you? I asked you a question."

I knew as soon as I opened my mouth it would lead to a verbal throw of words.

"Yeah, I heard you. What do you want me to say? Kyron and I have years together. You should expect that his family is gonna act this way. They know how much Kyron loves me." Didn't I strike a mothafuckin' nerve when I said that. Tomiere was speeding out of control not even paying attention to the road.

"That ma'fucka don't love you. He loves the dick that's in his cell every night!"

It was one thing to make an ill comment, but to call Kyron gay – *hell no*! Little did he know him saying that didn't change one damn thought about my feelings for Kyron. In fact, more and more I was praying that Kyron would still be in my life. We did have a child together. He couldn't exactly run out of my life just like that.

"Listen, you don't have to belittle Kyron to make me think less of him." I had to be the morally superior person since he was acting like a total ass.

"Fuck that. How I know that's even my baby?" lamely, Tomiere voiced.

"I'm not goin' there with you. Let's just go back to your crib and relax. I'm tired and I'm hungry." I was more than that though; I was agitated and depressed.

"How about I drop you off there and you can relax," he volunteered.

"Whatever, let's just make it happen."

Tomiere pulled up to his complex and passed me the key to the house. I was desperately relieved that he wasn't coming in with me. Nobody wanted to hear his fuckin' mouth. I felt the lack of trust ascending in the air when I exited the vehicle.

"Don't call those ma'fuckas on my phone either – neither one of them!"

I turned the key to open the door to get inside as he watched and fussed. He didn't control a damn thing like he thought he did. I would call any got-damn body I wanted to on his phone – both of them! How stupid was he? Stupid enough to come inside the house after he'd been gone all day and press redial on the phone hoping he'd luck up on another man's number. I wasn't that damn dumb.

I remember I'd called my mom's house one time and afterwards I called my bank to check my balance. This fool thought I had a special code to my mom's voicemail! I didn't even have access to Ella's shit. That's what jealousy and the lack of trust will do – drive you up the fuckin' wall. That or it was his conscience that was eating at him because he was doing me wrong. Then, the way we linked up was foul so it wasn't unusual that he didn't trust me. Nothing about us was real, except for the money.

After he left from in front of the house, I made myself comfortable in his living quarters. With his heritage, he embraced both cultures. His mother was a Latina woman, but his father was 100% negro. I hadn't inquired much about them because they lived miles away in Phoenix, Arizona. Tomiere didn't have any other family members living in Delaware. He was the only one that chose to stay when his mother and father relocated. There were many photos of them posted around his living room. Along with a beautiful pencil shadowed portrait of his gorgeous mother.

I sat on my favorite sofa bed and pulled out a spiral notebook that was inside the coffee table next to the sofa to write a letter to Kyron. I had to explain to him how sorry I was for fucking up. He didn't deserve to hear it from anyone else. Although, I knew he would. I prayed that he would call me during the times I was home so I could explain it. After taking my time to write the letter and eating, I ended up falling asleep.

"What the fuck is this?"

I could barely open my eyes before Tomiere was in my face. It was the letter I'd written to Kyron. I wasn't about to explain my apologies to Kyron, to him, so I sat myself up.

"It is what it is. Now, can you take me home?" I asked him.

He stood in a rejected space realizing that I still had love for Kyron.

"Nah man, I'm not taking you nowhere until you explain this to me."

As he towered over me, I could smell cheap perfume on him. I knew he'd dropped me off to go see another woman. Yet, he wanted me to explain why I apologized and told the love of my life that I fucked him over and was very regretful that I did. I begged Kyron in my letter to have an understanding ear and to please keep a warm heart since I was his daughter's mother. Your heart doesn't lie and neither was I when I wrote that letter.

"I'll always have love for Kyron, Tomiere. I mean, you and I are not even that serious. You provide for me and I provide for you, simple as that. Ain't no love here. Both of us know that.

Yeah, you may have been the man that took my virginity, but that don't mean nothing compared to the love I have for Kyron. You need to realize that." I don't know where in the conversation I lost Tomiere, but it had to be when I said he took my virginity. This damn fool gripped me for dear life and began kissing all over me.

"I knew we were meant to be together. This is my pussy! I was the first to crack that open. Man, fuck that nigga, you mine."

My face was torn up and he was acting unnecessarily ridiculous. If I could've reversed my words, I would have. But it was too late. He finally let me go and ripped up the letter to discard it. He had to feel like the proudest man in the hood to know that he took my virginity. This boosted him up much more.

"Ain't no need to write him; he's through wit' you. You let me plant a seed in that. Do you really think he'll still want you? And, if he knows that I was the first to hit it, he'll never want you back now. Shit, I broke you in. All men have a problem with the first guy to hit it, unless it was him."

What woman ever tells another man about the first guy to hit it unless it was him? Definitely not me, what was the relevance? And shit, in my mind yes, Kyron and I would always be together. It didn't matter that he ripped up my letter. I'd write another one.

Yes... it's true

"Medina please open up this got-damn door!" I banged louder each time I asked her to let me in. Medina was another person on my, "angry at Serenity" list.

"Why didn't you do it, Serenity?" she asked me looking from behind her curtains like I was contagious and she didn't want me in her house.

"Scabby!!" I yelled, "Tell Medina to open up this fuckin' door!"

"He's not home, so don't even call his name."

"Medina, open the damn door, now!"

Pretending to pout she came to the front door, but only cracked it open.

"We can talk from here."

I was now six months and had lied to Medina and told her I was getting an abortion. The first conversation we had about me being pregnant was when I tagged along with her and Scabby to Friday's for a couple of drinks. That night every drink the bartender made for me tasted funny. Now, Medina was every step of the way with me with Dalya and much like a concerned man she paid attention to my habits. I had missed my period for two months in a row and had begun to have strange cravings. I was often too tired to hang out with them when I got off of work and she noticed. That particular night, I couldn't hold my liquor. Not from being drunk, but because it wouldn't stay down. I ended up between two bathroom stalls throwing up all the liquids that were inside of me.

"Bitch, you pregnant!" she called me out when I came back to the bar. "Look at her, Scabby. Her face is filling out and that heifer's put on weight."

For a woman that never had kids, she damn sure was a pregnantology expert.

I felt so weak and drained, that I planted my face on the bar. Scabby lifted up my chin.

"You ain't let old boy knock that up did you?"

I knew my body. At that time I certainly hoped I wasn't pregnant, but then, I knew I was.

"I think I fucked up, Scabby." I began to cry.

"Let me beat her ass, Scabby! MOVE!"

Medina was so frustrated with my actions. She was steady trying to push Scabby out the way while he consoled me.

"Damn, Serenity!" Scabby cursed. "Why you let him hit it raw? You so damn *hardheaded*. What you gon' do?"

Here we were making a scene in TGIF's on a packed Friday evening.

"I'm not keeping it." I softly responded, too unsure of my own answer.

"Good!" Medina yelled. "Kyron don't need to stomach that while he's in the bing. Get a fuckin' abortion and be done with Tomiere if you ever want to get Kyron back. Tomiere ain't being loyal to you no how. Ask Urs about that! Kyron is the best damn thing that ever happened to you."

"Medina, relax. It's her decision. Not every woman wanna kill a baby."

My throat was parched and I was trapped in Scabby's space, even feeling the tenseness in his body as he held me. I heard more footsteps around me and tried not to make a big deal of this.

"Like she needs another damn baby. You gon' get an abortion and that's my word!" Medina stated like she was a mother talking to her teenage daughter with no sense of gratitude that God granted the gift of life.

"Let's bounce." Scabby saw the way the waitresses and the waiters were huddled together glancing in our direction. "I think they're about to put us out anyway."

Medina and I had a long conversation about it and after her drilling me, I promised her I'd get an abortion. *Scabby voted against it.*

"Don't ruin your life. You know you're my girl and I wouldn't steer you in the wrong direction. But if you have this baby, you can forget about Kyron." She wanted this to sink in my head. "Look at it this way, if you have the baby, Kyron will never forgive you. It will be a constant reminder for him that you cheated." Coming from a woman who was more fascinated with living the single life this wasn't helpful advice. What woman would abort their baby because of what another person thought? Especially, a man sitting behind bars. Was that fair? To me, it wasn't. I'd contemplated on aborting the baby because I knew I wasn't a good parent to my first child. Hell, I never had her. Yet, I was about to bring another baby in this world. Lawd, help me!

"I'll make the appointment and go with you if you need me to," she offered.

"What should I tell Tomiere? This would be his first child." Outside the circumstances that he'd be pissed, I was also worried about how I'd feel. I'd never had an abortion before. Could I really go through with it and carry on like I hadn't taken part in killing a baby? Just my luck though, I'd be in that small percentage where I'd die in the process of having the fetus sucked out of me.

"Fuck a Tomiere. What about him? I wouldn't give a fuck if he never had a child. Tell him to knock up one of his other bitches." Medina was so cold and heartless sometimes.

"I don't know if I can go through with it. How did you?"

This is the part I never understood about her. All of those years her and Scabby had been together, she'd had two abortions and two miscarriages. And judging from her behavior, I doubt if those two miscarriages were accidental. Medina clearly didn't want kids.

"Easily. I spread my legs open and let the professionals do what their J-O-B! I know how bad my man wants a child, but I also know he's not really ready. The day he leaves the streets alone for good, then, I'll know. I wouldn't dare bring a baby in this world to struggle with me. You know how Scabby's in and out of jail. Why would I do that to myself?"

She made her point, but it wasn't that easy for me.

"Schedule the appointment," I said, passively. "I'll go, but I'd rather do it alone." I knew if she went with me, I'd go through with it and deep down I really didn't wanna do it.

That's why she was so mad at me. She'd scheduled the appointment, but I never went.

"I see why men can't trust you; you lie too much," she confessed, finally opening the door to let me in.

I expected our conversation to change once she sympathized with the extra 30 pounds I'd already gained, but nope, it didn't. This bitch was heartless.

"You had up until this month to get rid of it, but you didn't. Don't ask me for a single line of advice either when this shit blows up in your face because it will. I don't want to hear it when it does."

I followed behind Medina into her basement where Scabby and a few other guys, including JaQuill, were playing cards. My heart fluttered when I laid eyes on him.

"Hell no! I'm out of here." JaQuill pulled back the metal and blue fabric table chair and threw his hand in.

"Hey y'all." I tried to act non-caring and spoke like usual when I entered a room.

"You betta slow up eating, girl. You gettin' big and not just your belly either," Scabby blurted in front of everyone.

With barely audible emotions, I became engrossed with tears.

"Fuck her!" I heard JaQuill say to Medina. "This ho deserves to cry. My cousin is in jail crying over this slut trying to get in his last 15 months. This tramp is making it hard for him."

His words made me cry outwardly now. I was an emotional wreck. One of Scabby's other partna's turned to me and said, "Yo! Y'all can you take that shit upstairs. It's money on the line!"

Out of distress, I did as he suggested. I went upstairs into the earthy beige, burgundy and hunter green tone living room and plopped down on the couch. Their house didn't have nare sign of a child. It was suited for the two of them.

Medina hadn't come back upstairs and I had dozed off for nearly two hours. My best friend was even separating and becoming distant with me because I was pregnant by Tomiere. It wasn't like I cheated on her. What did she care? Or, was it the principle of me doing it? *I don't know.* I had a dark cloud over me that refused to turn into sunshine.

That night instead of going home, I spent the night over my mother's house. When Ella opened the door, the weariness around her eyes and crevices of her mouth showed me that she was aging. *Damn! I took part in that.* I imagined I helped her age by leaving my responsibility on her hands. It felt fucked up because once again, I was about to do it again.

"Kyron just called here for you. He said he's been calling your house, but you're never home. Where have you been staying?"

Ella didn't involve herself in my business, but from her experience with my father, she knew what I'd done could produce the same results.

"You know you can't keep running from him, Serenity. You were woman enough to get pregnant by his friend, now shouldn't you be woman enough to talk to him about it?"

I collapsed my tired body against the wall leading to the stairs. "Mom, I'm tired. I'm going to bed."

I was so sick of everybody telling me what I should do. The only three people who were in favor of me having this baby were Tomiere, Scabby and me.

Even though it seemed useless, I began to gravitate toward Tomiere and was willing to comprise my life by building on nothing.

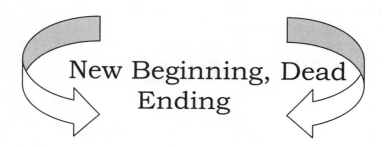

New Beginning, Dead Ending

It was two months since I'd even given birth to Tashee, my beautiful mulatto princess. She came out the womb with her father's unique characteristics. She even had the same dimple in her left butt cheek as he did. Tomiere had to be prouder than Kyron was when Dalya was born. He put an announcement in the local newspaper along with the one picture we took together. Didn't that fly through our small little city and the jail cells?

About a week after the announcement was in the paper, I received a not so nice letter from Kyron. He started the letter off like this... *Run into wisdom, power and peace.* That was the only inspirational line of the entire letter.

Serenity, the last time I checked my database you were working hard, taking care of our daughter and maintaining "our" place. Damn, so things have changed! First, you stopped answering my calls when I know you were looking dead at the caller ID. I guess that's when money was being exchanged for your services. You let Tomiere play you and cause you to betray me. Me... me, Serene. You betrayed me! I'm limp over this shit. That nigga was a closet supporter. As soon as the heat was on, he hid in the closet and didn't rightly own up to his part that he played. He knows the rules to the game. Then, you let him take you away from me. How can I ever look at you? Huh? The beauty that I once seen in you is deaded! Do you realize how much damage you've done? I thought you were my best friend. I guess I don't know my friends very well because I've been burnt by all of you. I had to learn the hard way: a friend is a good enemy because they know what buttons to push to take you over the edge. You've successfully done that. I've been dealing with it too, but to put a blast in the paper was shittin' and wiping my face with that same shit paper.

I quivered from the bitter cold of his letter as I read on. The only time he called me Serene was when it came from the depths of his soul.

That's cool though. At least Pumpkin remained my down ass bitch, when I thought you were. I'm glad that I hadn't cut her off. If I had, I'd be left for dead. I haven't received anything from you in the last year. You cut me off for the nigga partly responsible for putting me in here. That's ai'iight. I'ma do the last of my bid like a ma'fuckin' warrior! When I touch base the only hollering you gon' do is when I smack the fuck outta you! You better learn the game that you're playin'.

I started to haul-ass like Ella did! Instead, in less than 24 hours, I immediately changed my locks and gave my landlord my 30-day notice. Not that Kyron couldn't find me, but I thought I'd be safer at my mom's crib. I rented a storage space and put all of our furniture in there, with the exception of a few things. I called Ella and asked her if she minded if I came back home to live. Tomiere had stopped passing off as generous as he did anyway just before Tashee was born. He wanted me to move in with him, but I wasn't about to set myself up like that.

Tashee and I did stay with him most nights though, until my mom decided she wanted her other grandbaby with her too. That was inevitable.

Tashee was six months when I packed her bags. Tomiere was against it and told me if I shipped Tashee away I might as well go with her because that's the only reason why he let me live with him. So, I also packed up my stuff and left. All that I jeopardized for him and he called himself putting me out? Straight evicting me from his crib – sucka ass ma'fucka!

This news quickly became the talk of the town when Tomiere's bitch ass placed another announcement in the paper, but this time it said, "Nothing Lasts Forever" with the same picture of him and I except, the picture was placed inside of a broken heart. I was the laughing stock of the Gate.

The circumstances surrounding me going home were petty. Tomiere acted real childish, behaving like one because I suggested that Tashee would be better off living with Ella. It was drugs kept in his place and it wasn't right to jeopardize my life, let alone, our child's. It was foolish of me to even stay there, but that was the risk I took.

Since I was laid off of work, I wasn't able to keep up on the bills and a truck payment. I was only receiving a mere $222 per week in unemployment benefits. How ironic was it that things were going back the same way they were when Kyron first went to jail? Now that he was on his way home, I was busted. The truck was about to be repossessed if I didn't do something about it. So, I came up with the scheme to fraud the insurance company... total it, steal it, what-the-fuck-evah to get that paper. I got up with Scabby and asked him to hook it up for me.

"If I do this for you, you gotta promise me that you'll split the scrilla with Kyron since this was his truck." With his sharp chiseled features and shaved facial hair, Scabby unfolded his arms and made me promise.

"I can do that. Just make it happen." It wasn't bullshit talk either. I would give Kyron his portion of the money. I was try'na win him back.

Scabby had the truck stolen and after reporting it to the Police and the insurance company, I received my check about two months later. After depreciation, I still came out with a hefty check. I took my half of the money and put Kyron's up. Besides, the truck was in both of our names. It was only right to give him his half. I'd decided that, that money was my peace offering to him.

Coming of Age

I'd been back home for three and a half months lying around the house in sweats about to cook me something to eat to stop my hunger pains. My mom had taken the girl's along with her to a church function, so I was left alone. I really had to do something about my situation. You know, get my life back in order. I searched inside the freezer to get the steak-ums to fix me a nice cheesesteak with fried onions on one of those soft steak rolls my mom had in her pantry. I grabbed the bag of raw onions and pulled out the smallest onion I could find to slice it. I placed the cut up onions in the iron skillet that was under low flames. I heard the telephone ring, but I didn't want to be bothered. It was probably only telemarketers ringing the hell out of the phone. The ringing continued so, finally, I answered it. This phone didn't have the caller ID on it so I didn't know who was on the other end.

Only a handful of people knew that I was back home and that included Medina and Scabby. Can you believe after all that talk and advertising Tomiere was on the phone begging me to come over? He hadn't so much as spoke to me when he would come to check on his daughter.

Or, when he picked her up for a little outing. I never let her spend the night with him if I wasn't there. Not because I didn't trust him, but because I didn't trust one of his professions. I figured he was calling because I fixed his ass for putting me out. I went to Family court to get paperwork for child support and mailed the blank copies to his house. I wanted him to get the picture – pay up or let the white man decide how much you should pay per month. I thought this was the reason he was calling me. I had my onions sautéed in the pan under a little butter. They smelled good and getting soft and brown. I couldn't wait to season my steak up and slap two or three pieces of cheese on that thing and some mayo on my roll. In my mind, I could taste how good the sandwich would be before I even took one bite. I wasn't thinking about Tomiere's ass.

"Yo! What you been doin'? I've been blowin' up your cell, why you ain't answerin'? *You busy?*"

"Tashee ain't here. She's with Ella at the church if you wanna get her." I immediately responded.

"I'm not calling for her. I'm calling to find out if I can come scoop you up."

"Oh, now you wanna fuck with me. Not after you played me like that in the paper." I couldn't wait to hear his excuse about why he did that bitch shit.

"You played me – I played you! I shoulda never caught you sneakin' with that dude, Lewis. Yo, Kyron know you was lettin' him hit? You scandalous! They on the same football team."

"Nah, nigga... it wasn't just Lewis. It was Dabee, too. Get it right! You shoulda never put me out."

"Regardless of all that, can I come through? I received your packet of information and I wanna work a lil' sumpt'n out with you."

I figured, *why not?* Money was involved.

"I'm getting ready to eat, but swing pass in an hour and I'll be ready." I didn't rush to eat or get dressed for him; I took my time. I dressed casually and threw my hair in a quick ponytail. I heard the Titan pull up in front of the house with Jay Z's, *Song Cry,* coming out loudly from the speakers. I grabbed my handbag and darted out the door.

"Let me see 'dat thang from the back. Show me what it do," Tomiere smiled, with his handsome self. Even while I was disappointed with him, I could hardly ever resist his charming ways.

"It closed up for you," I cut my eyes.

"I guess I have to bust that thing open again," he charmingly smiled again.

This was all this was about, him getting in between my legs.

"Somebody's horny I see." I glanced down in his lap where his right hand should've been on the steering wheel but it wasn't, it was in between his legs.

"Nah, this is about this." He threw the family court papers at me from the side of his door.

"What about it? Pay up or go deal with them. That's all to it." I had been a hustle bunny for him too long without still reaping the benefits and I had a baby for him. Uh uhn, he still had to come out his pockets.

"I got you. Don't I always?"

"Not lately. If you had, I wouldn't have to go this far."

"Let me see ya phone."

I retrieved it from my handbag and gave it to him. Right kindly, he snatched it from me.

"You ain't gettin' it back either! You ain't calling no other niggas on the phone I'm payin' for."

"Stop playin', Tomiere and give me my phone back!"

"Okay, get in the truck. Let's take a ride. Depending on how you act, I may give it back to you."

*****

We pulled in front of his house and I expected the norm... for me to get inside the house, fuck his brains out and put him to sleep. That's exactly what happened, except when I woke up in the middle of the night with just a thin lace thigh-high negligee on, I was left alone. I got up and called out to him, but got no response – Tomiere was gone. I searched for the remote control to turn on the TV to find out what time it was – 1:32AM. I heard the wind from the front door opening and waited for Tomiere to come up the steps. Instead, what I saw complicated my life more than it had been. It was two guys dressed in all black wearing black ski masks. One of them I could see was brownskin and the other was very dark with a big ass forehead. Both were toting guns – big guns – pointing directly at me when they reached the top of the steps. The worse had yet to happen. I swear it was a dark cloud raining on my life.

I tried to cover up and scramble for safety. Tomiere's house was being robbed without him being there! I was so thankful that my daughter wasn't there, but where in the hell was Tomiere to save me?

There was a dark hate and an evil aura that these two men came in with.

"Where is the money and the coke bitch?"

Big bad me had the tongue snatched right outta my mouth. I jerked from trembling so badly. The brownskin man came closer to me and snatched the pillow I was holding onto for dear life that I used to conceal my nakedness.

Oh shit! I thought.

"Bitch, where is the shit at?" he mumbled disguising his voice. With his gun, he traced it around my face while the other man rummaged through the closet and the dressers in search of money and drugs.

Shaking and still silent in fear, I felt the eyes of a demon scouring my body. This ma'fucka was about to rape me; *I knew it! I knew it!* My heart hit the tip of my toes when I realized what he was about to do.

Oh God no! I thought in my head praying that Tomiere would come home any minute to save me. I thought of Kyron and what he told me when he was in the game. "Always keep a gat under the bed in case niggas run up in ya crib." I wondered if Tomiere held true to that same rule.

I felt my hands drop to the side of me in a panic to feel under there. I faintly heard the other guy say, *"Bingo!"* from finding money and plastic bags full of cocaine. I used that split second when the brownskin man turned his head to make my move. This was the second of truth. I was gonna blast these bastards if the gun was under there. I felt my hand digging, fishing, but coming out empty.

Damn!

Was Tomiere a true hustla? Where was his gat when I needed it?

The scene became completely different now. I was defenseless.

The one lustful man came toward me again, but this time enraged yanking me by the hair and shoving me forcefully to the floor.

"You lying bitch!"

I hadn't even said anything to them because I was too scared. How could he call me a liar?

"Where does he keep the rest?"

The rest meaning more money, more drugs, but I didn't know. When I didn't answer, both of them stood over me.

"Should I shoot the bitch?" The darker big forehead man asked like he needed the permission from the other bastard. I saw him nod "no" and I became relieved thinking I was about to get away without harm. "But you can fuck her," followed out his mouth.

My body tensed up and I curled up as tight as I could, when I felt the rough hands trying to stretch me out. But both of them were too strong for me. When I wouldn't cooperate, the darker one held his gun to my temple.

"Bitch, I will blast you if you don't loosen up. I will split that dome in two."

Against my will, I submitted and allowed my body to fall limp. I watched as the brownskin man dropped his pants low, slouched down to his knees, and forced himself inside of me. I wanted to snatch that ski mask off of his face, but I didn't have the courage. Hot tears streaked down the side of my face while he was fuckin' the shit outta me.

Fucking with Tomiere had caused me more pain than me staying faithful to Kyron. A thousand regretful thoughts ran through my mind as my body jerked up and down from him ramming inside my pussy. I refused to gyrate or even move to encourage the pleasure that he stripped away from me. And, this nigga was putting it on me! What would Kyron think of me now? Would he think I was less than a woman not to scream? Would he say I deserved this because I put myself in this situation? Or, would he think I was damaged goods after the fact? The thoughts challenged each other for answers.

After I felt the hot semen ease from me, the thought of this invader having HIV and other diseases rocked me. Still, with a gun to my temple, I wanted to live! So many women tried to play hero and even though one or two of them are blessed enough to get free, hundreds of them aren't. I didn't want to be in that statistic.

The darker man switched places with the brownskin guy, but he was clever about his infiltration. He pulled one of Tomiere's condoms from the dresser that we never used and put it on him before he began damaging me. All this time had passed and no Tomiere to the rescue. I vowed to myself to never fuck with him again. Baby or no baby, by him! When he was finished abusing and tearing out my insides, he rose from me and kicked me harshly like trash.

"That pussy ain't even good as niggas say it is!"

What the fu--! These niggas knew me. I heard the brownskin dude come in my pussy's defense.

"That pussy was hot and ready. You had to hit that thang raw."

They both laughed as if their violation hadn't insulted me.

"Get in the closet and don't bring ya ass out until we're gone!" The darker man hollered lifting me up aggressively with his foot.

I jumped up and rushed into the closet for dear life. I had to be in that closet for at least twenty minutes before I finally came out.

My first response was to call the cops regardless if there were drugs in the house. I had been violated and I wanted them to help me. I scrambled for my clothes and the phone. Never once did I think getting sexy for my man would lead to this. If I had been covered up, maybe they wouldn't have raped me. That was my thought.

Once I got off the phone with 911, they instructed me not to wash because it might destroy DNA. I hit Tomiere's cell about a hundred times only to get his voicemail.

His phone was off.

The Police didn't arrive until 3:58AM, too damn long after the incident occurred. Tomiere still hadn't shown up or called me back from all the messages that I left him.

It was two officers: one black male – Officer Ryan, and one white female – Officer Talbert, that came to the scene to fingerprint and ask me 101 questions. They didn't seem too concerned about the rape. That shit bothered me. Their main concern was why the men thought it was money in the house. They kept asking me if I had made this up because my man hadn't come home. Or, the common stereotypical question – was he a drug dealer. I was pissed the fuck off at their line of questioning! I knew some women lied about being raped, but how far would they go? I had DNA dried up on my inner thighs and moisture still between my legs. What did I have to do, spread my legs open wide for them to scrape it out of me? Bastards!

Thirty minutes of going back and forth with them Tomiere decides to at last show up. He didn't look one bit surprised by the cops being there. In actuality, this nigga was too calm and had me wondering if he plotted on me.

"Why the fuck didn't you answer my calls?" All of that hidden silence was now gone and rage spoke for me.

The cops never pressed Tomiere, but now that they were in his personal space, he felt violated.

"Bitch, why do you have the fuckin' cops at my crib?" he asked so forcefully, disrespecting me which let me know he was afraid and there were most likely drugs in the house. His bitch ass had to pay for all of this. Now, I knew he probably did live by the rule of having a gun under his bed, but he probably removed it so I would be powerless. I blamed the rape on him and my response let him know that.

"I have them at your fuckin' crib 'cause you are a drug dealer and have drugs up in here!"

Officer Ryan eased his hand on his gun as Tomiere plunged toward me.

"Why are you lying to them like that? What is, this a fuckin' set up?" He couldn't believe I came out my mouth to tell them that. *Why not?* He had ruined my life and it was time to ruin his!

I heard Officer Ryan call for backup and the canine unit. Officer Talbert took me out of earshot of Tomiere and her partner.

"If what you're saying is true, you may also be charged. Do you understand this?"

Her grip was strong and forceful. My guess was that she thought this was some sort of game – payback maybe.

"I'm not being charged for a damn thing. I'll get up on the stand and testify first before I go down for him."

He did Kyron in and I wouldn't have a problem doing him in – fuck him!

"We can deal with that after he's been charged. If he even gets charged. For now, I'll take you over to the hospital trauma unit where a Doctor will conduct an examination."

Now that I'd finally given up some information that could benefit them, they were now trying to attend to my needs.

She took me back in the room where Tomiere was being held. I paused and slowed down walking pass him. Now, he was the one speechless. The closer I came to him, the more rage built up inside of me. Without remorse, I slapped his face so hard, red speckles flushed throughout his jaw.

I didn't know how I was going to rebound from this, but somehow I knew I would. I was a survivor.

I Will Survive

The closer it came to Kyron coming home, the less fearful I became. No matter if he slapped the taste out of my mouth, I was going to ride with him. This was one time I'd give him a "hit me" pass. I deserved it. I wanted my man back plain and simple. Whether or not Kyron wanted to hear from me, my guilt made me write him a long letter. A part of me had been taken away the day of the rape, but I truly believed you have to lose a part of you to make yourself whole. That incident instantly made me change (at least temporarily). No longer was I boastful nor did I feel beautiful anymore. Anytime I could let two men violate me and not scream, fight or pull out any defense mechanism to help me, how could I? I had been stripped physically and emotionally. I know Kyron probably didn't give a fuck. Hell, he probably thought I deserved what happened to me for being so fresh. I began to feel that God had punished me for betraying him. I couldn't feel his pain, but I did feel the torment of having someone take advantage of me when I was in a vulnerable position. I mistreated Kyron when he was down and out so I assumed this was my payback.

In my letter, I kept expressing how sorry I was and I'd hoped he'd forgiven me. I didn't want to share with him about the rape, but the victim in me wanted sympathy, so I did so, hoping he would show compassion for me. Possibly, want to console me for having been put through that unforgettable ordeal. I never told anyone about it at this point, not even Ella or Medina. In fact, I knew I wouldn't share this with my mom.

After I sealed his letter, I walked over to the mailbox. I could see Scabby coming out the house with a blunt dangling from his mouth.

"Hey girl," he uttered. "Come 'ere."

Lazily, I walked over to him in my pajama pants, house slippers and a silk scarf tied tight around my head.

"You know better coming outside the crib like that."

Little did Scabby know I wanted to hide in a room and not face the world from my grief. Not even my mother or my daughters could raise my spirit.

"I'm not trying to press nobody." I watched methodically how he inhaled the smoke and I yearned to do the same. "Let me hit that blunt." He took it from his mouth and handed it to me as I sat down on their steps.

"When you start puffin'? Damn, you really got turned out when ya man went to jail. That other nigga even got you snitchin'. I can trust that you won't call the cops on me, can't I?"

With his drawn conclusion of me, my heart felt an aching pain as I defended my actions. I pulled in about three times deeply before exhaling and didn't even choke off that good green when I did it. When I finally exhaled, smoke stretched out of my mouth. I needed to temporarily be relieved so I kept the blunt. I didn't even pass it back to him.

"I've done many of things, but Scabby, you my nigga. You know I would never drop dime on you. I had my reasons for telling on that bitch-ass nigga. You should know me better than to volunteer info to the police. I don't get a percentage of the raise from bustin' a hustler. I've always lived by the code. Kyron taught me that. Now, I may have slipped with the code of staying 'true to ya man' when he goes down, but does that make me that bad? Niggas fuck up all the time when they're not in jail and women take them back 99.8% of the time." I began to analyze my situation making me feel better. "I don't care that Tomiere got arrested. My only concern is that now he's in jail with Kyron. Kyron has to suffer more because I know how proud Tomiere is. I bet he's running off at the mouth about banging me and snatching me up from him. It's my stupidity though. I allowed it to happen. Now, Kyron and I will probably never get back. I fucked up my life, Scabby."

Scabby had pulled out another blunt and lit it. I seen him reach inside his pants pocket and pull out a clear plastic bag full of pills.

"Here, smoke some and take two of these pills. It will help you deal with that pressure."

Like a true dealer, Scabby was trying to help temporarily fix my misery. He wasn't trying to get me hooked; he only wanted to help out. You know, start me off. He called Medina to the door and asked her to bring out two bottled waters. When Medina came outside she blasted on me.

"You look a wrecked mess. I knew it was you out here spilling ya guts to my man. When y'all done talking come inside, I wanna talk with you."

"Ai'ight." I needed to talk to her too, but I needed to talk to Scabby more to get a male's point of view.

"Make sure you drink that water with those pills so you won't get dehydrated."

I didn't even ask him what kind of pills they were; I just took them. Whatever they were they would help me deal with my depression.

"Tell me the truth, Scabby... do you think Kyron will ever forgive me?"

Scabby exhaled smoke and lowered his eyelids. "Damn, baby, I don't know. You put a nigga in a tough spot. Straight took his manhood and displayed it in front of everybody. Unless he takes his negatives and makes them a positive, he may never forgive you."

My head dropped back in defeat and I placed one pill down my throat and chased it with the water to drug my life away.

"Kyron's a smart dude. He's hurt, but he's a rider. By now, he's probably doing 100 to 200 push-ups per day. Or, putting his head in non-fiction books try'na get his mind off of you. Damn, though Serenity," he paused. I could see the frustration come over him when he gripped his chin. "Now that Tomiere was fast tracked through the system and is in the same prison as Kyron, it will probably set a nigga back fo' real. The only way he can redeem himself is to get another female to ride with him. So, don't be surprised if he's corresponding with another dame."

That was not the response I wanted. I wanted him to say, "Ultimately, it's the love that will bring you two back together," but he didn't.

The enchanted feeling from the weed and the pills didn't stop me from crying. This would be a direct struggle to bring me back up to the woman I used to be. I thought about the letter I wrote to him. It had to be insulting to him that I had to involve the police when to him, Tomiere, was the police.

"So are you saying he won't fuck with me anymore?"

Scabby rubbed my scarf. "I'm saying it's a possibility that when he comes home he will stray another way." He was as real as he could get with me.

"He'll be home soon. What if I get myself together and show him I can be trusted, that I am the only woman for him," I asked, earnestly with a glimpse of hope.

"It's cool to do that, but do it for yourself and your kids, not for him, okay?" He kept rubbing my head trying to console me, as if to say, *Hell No!* He ain't coming back.

"You don't understand, Scabby. I need Kyron. You don't know what I've been through fuckin' with Tomiere." I gave him hints of my emotional trauma.

"Yeah, but do you know what Kyron's been through and going through because of you and him? They are in jail together. Tomiere might fuck around and start some shit because Kyron's time is about up. Kyron has to stay on point to get out the bricks. You don't think it's more of a challenge for him right now? Seeing Tomiere everyday is a constant reminder of you and he's trying to erase those memories to do his time. You better hope Tomiere don't do nothin' stupid to get Kyron more time. He'll hate you if that shit happens. You do realize niggas get killed over bitches."

I felt my body become sluggish and began to cry again, but this time I cried dry tears.

"Scabby, I got raped by two dudes the last time I was over Tomiere's house. That's why I alluded to the cops he had drugs in there. But I didn't know how much since, the dudes found his hiding spot. I think he set me up."

"Awe shit, Serenity!" Scabby cursed the demons. "Let me get Medina, I can't help you with this one. Medina!" he yelled and she came out. "Take ya girl in the house. She needs to talk with you." He helped get me off the steps. Hugged and assured me, "I'll find out who they were and they'll get dealt with."

I went inside the house tormented by what I'd become – a basket case. The only feeling that calmed me was weed and pills. If I had to smoke and pop pills everyday I would to deal with my pain.

This was my introduction to a life of "get high", all thanks to Tomiere.

After the Love is Gone

Nothing had gone as I predicted before Kyron was released from jail. Even though I had a baby on him, I'd cleaned up my act and prayed to God he would take me back even with the fact his last letter to me told me he wasn't. "Let's not waste anymore time than we have to. You wanted to leave me for another man. You had a baby on me. So, consider yourself free." Those were his exact words. Still, I prettied myself up knowing the exact date he was getting out and in my mind I knew there was no way he could reject me. I was the love of his life!

Scabby and Medina insisted that I didn't go, but I didn't take their advice. I took my hard earned money and rented a car to go pick my man up to take him away from that hell hole that he was in for 3 years. He was still my man as far as I was concerned – fuck what you heard! Yes, I was nervous and if you ever put a seashell up to your ear and listened to the steady wind blowing, that's how I was up to that point. The difference between the seashell and me was that the wind was blowing my body, not just whistling in my ear. I was trying to keep my balance to walk that straight line, but it wasn't easy. It was fucked up what I'd done to Kyron, no doubt, but I believed the love between us (well, his love now concealed deep down) would come to surface again.

I had not moved in the last few moments staring toward my mother's halfway open mini blinds in her living room window. When I did pick Kyron up, we didn't have a place of our own to stay. We would be back living at my mother's house. However, this time instead of a bedroom we'd have the basement all to ourselves, like that uncle that didn't wanna leave underneath his sister's wing. Dowsed in my thoughts, I hadn't heard my mom and my two girls come in from planting flowers in the backyard. Dalya came running to me first with her dirty covered hands.

"*Mommy!*"

Before she could reach me, I swatted her away. "Don't put those dirty hands on me," I warned, not wanting any smudges of dirt on my mango linen outfit that I'd purchased from the Macy's clearance rack. It was just about summer so I accented my outfit with flip-flops and a straw hat with a scarf around it that had multiple colors in it to help the deep orange color to stand out. This hadn't been one of my typical outfits since Kyron was gone. This was a classy get up to him. Really, any outfit that covered my body was classy to him. I allowed my blouse to remain open to expose my tank that was underneath it. My confidence had built back up some and the blunt I smoked helped that confidence.

My mother came in holding Tashee on her hip with her pastel housecoat halfway up her thighs.

"That's mom-mom's baby. Oh, yes she is," she glowed, warm and high spirited causing my little princess to smile with mostly gums and a few teeth cutting through.

My disapproval of Dalya coming to hug me caused her some disappointment from the way she pouted her way to hug my mother instead.

"Are you leaving out?" my mother inquired, her hands were covered in just as much dirt as Dalya's.

"Sure am. I'm on my way to pick up my man. Today is his max-out date."

My mother hesitated to respond and calmly sat Tashee in the playpen that was in between the living room and the family room.

"Dalya turn on Sesame Street for you and your sister."

I expected my mom to mind her business as she normally did. But not today! Her soft oval face frowned when she had the children leave the room. Ella loved me regardless to how she disliked my ways, but she sure in hell loved her grandbabies more.

"What man?" she asked, after the girls got situated.

"I only have one man, you know that."

"Serenity, the last man I've known you to have is that young man Tomiere. And, if you're going to pick him up, you can forget about him coming here." She never did feel that strongly about him. Kyron was her son-in-law in her eyes.

"To hell I am! I'm gonna pick up Kyron. Not no damn Tomiere." I skimmed over her face slowly.

"And, do you think that's even wise, Serenity? The last conversation you and I had about him you said he didn't want anything to do with you, has that changed?"

Distressing as it may have been, I lifted my chin up high, "Nope. But it will change once he sees me."

"Damn you, Serenity. Talking to you is like going around on merry-go-round. You talk in circles! Baby, don't be like me, I spent my 30's trying to correct my 20's. Don't make this mistake. What would make you think he wants to be bothered with you after you've hurt him?"

This was a positive, I thought sarcastically.

"Well, considering that everything I do seems abnormal to you, what I'm about to do isn't that unusual."

"It's not about what you think is right. In this case, you're skating on thin ice. Lord! What have I done that caused my daughter to turn out like this?"

The crevices of her mouth wrinkled and the sun glinting off the mini blinds beamed down on her. I walked up to her and gave her a tight squeeze on her arms. Her muscles clamped tight.

"Mom, I'm a grown woman. I can take care of myself."

"This is what scares me," she objectively uttered. "If it doesn't go as planned, I'm here for you. Remember if it's not His will, there's nothing you can do."

I paused, ignoring the possibility of being rejected by Kyron. My mother turned and readied herself to fix the girls something to eat. I heard their voices singing ABC's echoing through the family room. I decided not to bother them before I left. I removed my keys from the key rack and sashayed my way to the Dodge Intrepid rental car that I rented from Enterprise.

Outside I took in a mouthful of stale air. I'd prepared for this day to explain face to face to Kyron how bad I felt for letting him down. To let him know how foolish I felt embarrassing myself in front of everyone putting myself on Front Street. I pressed the button on the wireless remote to unlock the car door. I placed my handbag on the passenger's side and removed the few CD's I put in there to entertain me on the ride. I would've called Medina to talk, but Tomiere had confiscated my cell phone a while back and I hadn't purchased a new one since.

ᚱ ᚱ ᚱ ᚱ ᚱ

The parking lot was full of cars in the Correctional Center visiting area. I thought perhaps, just as usual, many family members (mostly women) were going to see their loved one. Nothing seemed strange or out of place except me. Flustered with jitters and somewhat skeptical, I parked the car and got out to check the bag of money in the trunk that I was going to surprise Kyron with. *This will make it better,* I thought. Money always made it better for me. I'd arrived an hour early just in case they'd let him go earlier than anticipated. I looked down at my beautifully pedicured toes and then to my manicured hands. Kyron loved a woman who was well maintained. My hair was in large soft curls flowing freely. Kyron hated when I wore ponytail pieces or tracks, so I let my natural shoulder length flow. Anxious wasn't even a word to describe how I felt. More like ashamed since I could remember when I was coming faithfully to visit him and was remaining true to him. I'd let him down. Hell, I'd let myself down and truly didn't know how he would respond. I'd hoped he knew that regardless to what I'd done, I did wholeheartedly love him; even with my flaws.

I hesitated a few steps before I made my way to the entrance of the prison doors. I could remember thinking; *I can't wait until the day when my man is released.* That was in the early stage of his sentence. Now the day had come and I knew my flirtatious behavior probably cost me my relationship with the only man I loved. My voice trembled when I arrived to the visitor's desk.

"Umm, aah, I'm here to pick up Kyron Wells."

This time, C.O. Bowman didn't grace me. I wish it had been, to see his reaction to one of the brothas being set free. However, it wasn't. I was graced by a sista who appeared confused.

"There's another young lady that's here to pick him up as well. Are you two together?" she asked, unknowingly.

My eyes fretfully scoured the room to see whom this "young lady" she was talking about. "Where?"

The guard searched around the room with me. "She must've gone into the ladies room."

Without turning back to her, I restlessly took off to the bathroom. Just as I was about to open the door, the force from her pushing and me opening the door caused us to meet eye-to-eye.

This bitch, Pumpkin! That's whom I faced.

As much as I disliked someone downing me, my discontent for her made me say ill things about her. Why was she here? It was obvious, but I didn't want to believe it was because Kyron wanted her to be there. Too jumpy and without remorse or the thought of getting arrested, I pushed Pumpkin back into the ladies room.

"What the fuck do you think you're doin' Pumpkin?" As crushed as I was, this hussy was relaxed and peaceful.

"I'm here to claim what's mine. That's what I'm doing."

She had the nerve to be dressed up in a little cute outfit and her hair was done, but it was fully weaved. If it served me right, she even had a little make up on to enhance her looks. Her hair, nails and toes were done as far as I could see. She was ready and prettied herself just like I had, to take Kyron home to rock his world.

"I don't know why you would do this to yourself, Serenity. You had your chance with Kyron, but you blew it. You had his heart, but now it's with me. He's coming home with me. I'm sorry it isn't going to work out like you planned. We're not teenagers anymore. Now please, be a woman about this. In fact, let's just let Kyron decide what he's going to do," she expressed with much confidence like she knew he would chose her.

I was crazy, but I wasn't that stupid. Getting locked up in a prison facility was a no-no because I wanted to beat her ass! I was determined that Kyron was coming home to me, so I accepted her challenge. I was the #1 woman in his life. I would always be the mother of his only child.

I pushed her again and the devil in me really wanted her to nudge me just a bit, so I could pound on her, but she was the bigger person about the ordeal walking away without reacting.

We came out the bathroom just in time to see Kyron being freed from his handcuffs and given a brown bag of his personal belongings. The female guard at the desk had to know something was up by the way she kept a close eye on both of us. I'm sure this wasn't the first time she'd seen two females bump heads over a man. Kyron had a solemn look on his face; wasn't a sign of a happy smile coming. I glanced nervously at him and over to Pumpkin, who was only three steps away. Both of us were waiting to see who he would choose. Struggling to hold my temper, every step forward Kyron made, I wanted to reach out and grab every inch of his 200+ pounds. It was as if he slowly prepared for this day. Even with the green get-out-of jail prison clothes, he was well groomed. His cut was dark and low, blended well. His eyes were twinkling with brightness. My eyes were red from stress and glued on him and his glued to mine. But what I read in his eyes was *why in the hell are you here*? Just for a millisecond I thought as they released him, he'd come to me.

This was it: the test of our love. Unlike Kyron or me, Pumpkin stood with her shoulders straight and her nose up in the air. She had a reason to. As viciously painful as it was, Kyron made his stride steps away from me towards her. Leaning in his direction, I reached to him, but he pulled away awkwardly to embrace Pumpkin, giving her a satisfying kiss. All the while he's staring at me, never saying anything. With every ounce of dignity I excused myself before adding the explosion of tears. I deserved just what he dished out. I deserved to be shown that when you hurt someone, expect to get hurt in return.

I left the correctional facility feeling depressed and defeated. Damn, how I wished I had a cell phone to call Medina. She might have said, "I told you so," but I needed to hear something. I made it to the rental and thought about the cash in the trunk. *Fuck him! He's not getting shit. He'll only spend it on her. I wish I would give it him,* I thought out of envy. Even if I wanted to give it to him, I wouldn't in front of her. I placed my head on the steering wheel still fighting the tears until they walked pass in search of Pumpkin's car. Once they got a safe distance from me, I put in Brian McKnight's first CD and played, *After the Love Is Gone,* and managed to make my way from the parking lot two cars behind them.

The one-mile road seemed more like five miles until we both reached the intersection. I watched as Pumpkin pulled into the Wawa. I decided to pull in behind them, red eyes and all. I had something to say to him. I was still the mother of his child; she wasn't. Their bond couldn't have been that strong.

Uninvitingly, I stepped out of the car and called to Kyron.

"Kyron, can I please talk to you for a minute?"

Pumpkin grasped tight to his forearm not wanting to let him go, holding a bag full of new clothes in her other hand, for him to change into. Optimistic about talking to me, he eased Pumpkin's arm off of him. It was that moment that I knew Kyron felt my pain of seeing him with another woman. Or, from the tragedy I'd been through. The way his eyes sorrowfully gazed into mine, I knew he felt some remorse.

"Let me change out of these clothes and I'll let you say your peace."

Pumpkin cheerfully rubbed his back handing him the clothes. Disregarding me, she felt up on my man like he was hers. Quietly and suspended in my emotions, I patiently sat on the hood of the car watching the back of their soles go into the store. They were a couple; that fucked me up. Damn! It was really over between us. Was the love really gone? Or, was this just for show? Was he only doing this to hurt me like I'd hurt him? I just couldn't believe we were over.

They took about 15 minutes in the store. I imagined he was prepping her for his conversation with me. He came out the Wawa convenient store brand new – laughing and grinning at her. I deliberately turned in the other direction. I couldn't take it. My vision was already dimmed because of the sunbeam bouncing from the hood of the car, frying my brains. I nonchalantly propped my back forward. Kyron stood there right in front of me with unexpressed feelings.

"So?"

All of a sudden I choked up extremely insecure. The man I could once say anything to, I couldn't get the right words out to say what my heart felt.

"This is what we've come to?" I had the nerve to say subconsciously testing him.

"Yo, get the fuck outta here with that shit! Where's your man and ya new baby?" He flipped on me knowing where Tomiere was, but he was being smart.

"I didn't come here to discuss that. And for the record, Tomiere's not my new man." My mind was wandering like a stray cat trying to find a home for the right words to say. Pumpkin was sitting in the driver's seat waiting uncomplainingly on him as we chatted.

"All of that pressure you put on me. The hardship you made me face. I already knew going in there, there was a chance that I might lose you, but I didn't know it would turn out like this. You had niggas coming up to me saying how foul you were. Then, I was receiving many letters about how you were buck wild out there and you expect me to receive you like nothing ever happened? To make matters worse, you had a baby on me!"

I couldn't hide from my past so I stood tall with smudges of guilt riddled over me. My defense against the heat that was coming from the sun and from Kyron's mouth was just to be still. I didn't know how he truly felt and hearing him express himself made me hurt more.

"Everybody knew we were together. You spit in my face and then smeared it in. The same dude that influenced my jail time and the same dude that came on my tier when he got up, bragging to the other inmates that he stole my business and my girl from me. Telling them that y'all had a family together and that you were only on loan to me because he was the first man to get up in that. And, you had me thinking I was the first! I had to endure that humiliation; it did more than hurt me. It tore me down. I loved you, Serene."

I had demoralized my man and the bitter wrath he felt lingered out.

"I can never be with you again. The love will always be there, but right now, I don't have love for you." He stooped forward and gave me the friendly forehead kiss. "I'm sorry for what happened to you. You're strong I know you'll be able to get over it. I'll be through to get my daughter later on. Just please respect I have to get situated with my lady, okay?"

His lady?

Talk about tore down, a rain of blows beat my body emotionally. I couldn't even find any kind words to say. He left me standing there stupidly and gracefully walked to "his lady's" car.

The Year Without Him

Sleep evaded my eyes. I called myself concentrating on getting it right – concentrating on trying to better myself. It wasn't happening. Whoever said that the sweetest revenge is success is a sucka for even making that fuckin' statement. The sweetest revenge is getting the person who hurt you, back! That's exactly what Kyron did.

Eventually, I changed my mind about his share of the money and invited him over to Ella's. When he finally made it over, I thought this would mend the hurt from our wounds, but it hadn't. Like Scabby said, he'd drawn toward another woman to make him feel like a man again. But, Pumpkin wasn't me. She could never be me. If he wanted to be with her, he would've selected her years ago. He didn't though. He chose me. I was his choice so I knew their courtship wouldn't last; it couldn't last. Then, I'd feel totally defeated and I wasn't willing to let that happen.

Bright-ass me, I decided to practice celibacy for once like I should've done when Kyron was in jail. The last sexual encounter I had was with the rapists. Perhaps, this influenced my decision to become celibate. I still felt dirty inside. I didn't want any man in my sacred place unless it was Kyron, but he didn't want it. I thought he would at least want to hit it once after coming home from doing a three-year bid, but he hadn't made any suggestions of it when he'd come to get Dalya. Or, when he came to get the money. Then, he mostly came with pie face monitoring his every move. Kyron had changed. He was refined and more reserved like he didn't have time for bullshit. I guess doing three years would make anyone change. I wasn't sure if he'd changed for the better though. I wasn't sure if I even liked who he'd become. He wouldn't let me in to learn the new him. Religion wasn't a factor in his change that was evident. Medina was telling me that she'd seen him and Pumpkin out a few times during social hour at a bar her and Scabby frequented, which let me know he wasn't that pure. His ass was back drinking. One thing that was becoming increasingly distracting was when Kyron came to my mom's house he wouldn't even speak to Tashee and that bothered me, but not enough to say something to him about it. His obligation was to Dalya, not her. That's how I dealt with it.

To get my mind off of things, my weed habit and pill popping increased. My appearance hadn't changed. I was still the radiant beauty on the outside; however, on the inside I was filled with muck. Dirty and used up, that's how I felt. I would see Kyron driving Pumpkin's 2005 white Impala LT around town and even when he came to get Dalya. I thought I'd be the type that refused my child to go over another woman's house, but I wasn't that petty. As long as my child was safe, I was cool with her spending time over there with her father. I didn't like it, but I dealt with it.

One night on a solo mission to catch a movie, Kyron and Pumpkin were there. Torturing myself, I sat three rows behind them. I would catch Kyron's hand slip around her neck and give her a light peck. I wanted to drop kick both of them in the back of their heads. Instead, I delicately placed my popcorn on the floor from the loss of appetite and caught another movie. I couldn't take being in their presence. Kyron was doing everything to internally punish me. It was bad enough that I didn't have a car and most of my money was going toward rental cars. This bullshit had to end, but what could I do to make Kyron leave Pumpkin? She had a new car, a crib, a college degree, a damn good paying job and stability. I had none of these things.

♟♟♟♟♟

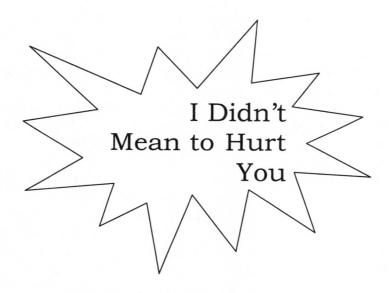

I Didn't Mean to Hurt You

Just when I was getting used to Kyron being out of my life, I received a call at home from Medina.

"You need to get over here now! Scabby's got the information you need."

I jumped up from my bed and turned off my television to rush over to Medina's house. With every word she said my heartbeat pounded in my ear. *What did they find out?* Soon as I got through the door I seen the hatred on Scabby's face, but not only his, Kyron's face was also distorted. Medina didn't tell me Kyron was in their house. I may have prettied myself up more to win favor with him. Now I truly wondered, *what was the stress of urgency?*

"Yo, I asked Kyron to come over here because he needs to discuss with you what I'm about to tell you."

I desperately needed a drag of the blunt Medina was smoking, but didn't want to smoke in front of Kyron if he disagreed. Since he'd come home I didn't know if he smoked or not. I knew he drank alcohol, but that was it.

"Sit down, Serenity," Scabby callously demanded. I used this moment to get close to Kyron by taking a seat next to him. I made sure my ass brushed against his hand before it landed on the cushion. I could smell the fresh scent of his cologne. I opened my nose wide and took long deep breaths to smell him to savor every second that I was near him. I could feel his broad shoulders next to mine when I scooted closer to him on the loveseat. The NY fitted that was turned to the back on his head was real sexy to me. Kyron had his bad boy image back. His swag was returning. I was in love all over again with my baby. Damn, he looked edible!

Scabby was holding back the vital information until I became settled.

"All of us know the ordeal you've been through. You came to me like a sister should when you needed help. You know we've always been there for you, Serenity. You're blood to both of us. Regardless if a nigga loves you or not, we're always here for you and have your best interest at heart." Scabby verbally bullied Kyron to let him know that even when a man turns their back on me, he and Medina still had my back.

"I know that." I backed him up on his statement.

"I know you know that, but Kyron needs to know this. We are the ones that had to console you when you came crying day after day about him making the choice to be with that other dame. I realize it was his decision and what you did to this man was fucked up. How many times have I told you this?" This was his way of letting Kyron know he spoke positive on his behalf.

I couldn't deny that he hadn't warned me.

"A lot." I tightened my lips.

"Some things you brought upon yourself, but I don't feel any woman deserves to be raped. I wasn't raised like that."

Medina was standing behind her man like a queen giving him moral support.

"No woman does!" she agreed, holding three rolled blunts in her hand and one she was starting to burn.

"That's why no matter what another man has done, it isn't in the code of street ethics for a nigga to take pussy behind the revenge on the next man."

My thoughts ascended to the air. *Where was he going with this*?

"*Ain't that right*, Kyron?" Scabby asked him.

Instead of faking like I didn't smoke, I said fuck it and reached my hand out for the blunt Medina had lit. To my surprise, after I inhaled three times, Kyron stuck his hand out for it.

Scabby continued, "You should've never been a victim of revenge, but you were, Serenity."

I was left out in the cold at a vulnerable moment.

"What!" I spewed in confusion.

Kyron's arm slid around me to hold me like he had when he and Pumpkin were in the movies. Passively, he began stroking my forearm. I longed for his touch, but instinctively I nudged him off of me.

"Kyron had two niggas run up in Tomiere's crib to rob him. Ain't that right, Kyron?" Scabby lit the blunt that was dangling out the corner of his mouth like he was lighting a cigarette.

My face slowly turned to him because I didn't want to believe that *my man* was the root behind this.

"Kyron?" I wasn't easily shocked, but this was shock-worthy.

"How was I to know you'd be there? Serenity, you can't blame this on me. Isn't it bad enough you were still fuckin' wit' that nigga?"

"Kyron, I was raped! I wrote you and told you how that shit made me feel. You never wrote me back or even acknowledged that you were the one that sent somebody up in there. All this time and you knew who it was! No matter how you feel about him, I am your baby's motha! You owe it to me to tell me who the low-life bastards are that stripped me of my womanhood and took ya pussy!"

I couldn't control myself. My fingers were pointed all in his face, but he still wouldn't tell me. Not once did I think it was somebody that I knew. Even though they knew me. So, I screamed, "WHO WAS IT, KYRON? YOU GOT SOMETHIN' TO HIDE?"

"Don't we all?" he turned to me and remarked crudely.

"You made me a victim of sexual abuse. Who was it, Kyron?" Doubtful and full of complaints, I'd drawn a magnet of trouble that wouldn't demagnetize from me. My feet pounded on the wooden floor as Scabby and Medina let us distressingly air out our differences. In between my thrilled shouts and sweat, without zeal, Kyron let me know the answer to my question drawing us together by a tragedy.

"Serene, I'm sorry baby. It was JaQuill and one of his niggas. Ah, Jermaine," his head slumped down in humiliation. Internally, I knew he didn't make that O.G. call for them to violate me, I could see it in his sincere eyes that he didn't. Yet, he knew all along and didn't say jack to me about it other than he knew I'd get over it.

My legs fell from under me and I plummeted to the floor. The brown-skin man with the disguised voice was JaQuill! He wanted to fuck me for years – fuckin' rapist! I bet the dark-skin man was the one that was with him that day I met up with Tomiere at the car wash. They had randomly acquaintance raped me. Someone they knew was in the right place at the wrong time. It didn't matter whether or not it was me, when an opportunity is presented to a rapist, he or she will attack and that's what they did. They attacked me in the midst of the robbery. That's what the rape crisis worker from the hospital explained to me. She said most women are date-raped while a small percentage of women are randomly raped. Well, in my definition, I was randomly acquaintance raped. JaQuill knew better than to do something like this, but what he didn't know was I was going to use this to my mothafuck'n advantage. Yes, I would "get over it" as Kyron so plainly stated, but he was about to do this bid with me... the bid of the after affects of being raped.

I balled my eyes out on the floor of Scabby and Medina's living room. Kyron fell down to the floor with me apologizing for what happened.

"I didn't want to believe you when you said they raped you in the letter. Apart of me didn't want to believe that my cousin would do such a thing. I'm sorry for holding out on you this long, but you hurt me. I wanted you to hurt, too. I'm sorry, Serene. I've already confronted JaQuill about the ordeal. His boy disappeared: nobody has seen him. I gotta tell you this though, I ain't mad that they robbed Tomiere's bitch-ass at all!"

I understood that part of it, as well.

"But you knew for an entire year!" I stretched out dramatically crying. "How could you do this to me? How could you, Kyron? You know how you said to me, *it's me... me, Serene*? That's how I feel now. It's me... me, Kyron, your baby momma that you got raped!"

Yes, I was truly hurt, but I utilized every drama lesson I was taught in theater class during high school to embellish the scene.

☑☑☑☑

That night Kyron didn't go home to Pumpkin: he stayed with me. My mom was so proud to see her baby Kyron back in the picture. She opened her arms wide to share her love.

"I knew you'd be back," she smothered him with her arms.

Dalya and Tashee came running to him and I noticed how he flinched somewhat when Tashee touched him like he didn't want her on him again.

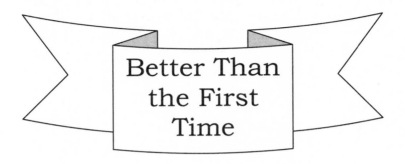

Better Than the First Time

Kyron and I sat quietly just listening to soothing music. Since the basement was the full length of the house, we had plenty of room. I'd adjusted to living down there and arranged it to my liking. The only real downside was the laundry room. I had to be subjected to the washing cycles and the spinning dryer. The upside to it was it was always a fresh scent brewing.

I'd placed my Brian McKnight CD in the CD player and put One Last Cry on repeat because I wanted Kyron to feel the agony of the lyrics that I felt when I rode home alone the day he chose Pumpkin over me. He had his back lain across the center of my bed with his arms interjected behind his head looking up to the ceiling. His large belt buckle was unfastened and his zipper to his jeans was midway down, completely exposing his boxers.

"How did we get here? Man, this is a fucked up situation."

I was unhurried to address his comment. Kyron was just opening up to me and I was anticipating his food for thought. I joined him on the bed, but I laid on my stomach.

"I'm sorry for what JaQuill did, Serene. That wasn't in the plan. Like I said, I'll deal with him again. I haven't been fuckin' with him like that since I came home and he told me the truth about what happened."

The music was to a minimum, however low enough to hear One Last Cry.

"JaQuill is your Aunt's son. How you gonna deal with him? He wanted to hit this since back in the day. He couldn't have me, so he took it and let his friend take advantage of me, too. What if I told you I want both of them dead? Would you do it? You said you'd take care of it."

Kyron rose up some with a startled stare. "I'd say you are fuckin' crazy! I ain't goin' back to jail for nobody. I'll square up with 'em, but kill 'em, hell no! JaQuill is my blood. Now, his boy, fuck him! I don't know why he let him in on it anyway." He spoke casually like I was cool with everything about his little plan.

"Blood or no blood, both of them violated me. I haven't been touched since they did that to me. Do you realize how scarred I am? It was scary enough that JaQuill went raw. I have to be tested every six months to make sure he didn't give me HI – fuckin' V! What woman wants to deal with that humiliation? That's the ultimate disrespect. I hate him and his boy for what they did to me. I can't even face them right now, but trust me, I want to." I slowly began to inch closer to him. It had been four long years in which I hadn't felt him inside of me. Of course I was troubled by my tragedy, but I longed for my man: His touch, his acceptance, his willingness to love me and not think that I was dirty on the inside. Right then, I wanted him to grip my ass, turn me over and slay me. Kyron was the cure to heal my pain.

I know he wondered why I hadn't mentioned anything about Pumpkin to him. Why would I? She wasn't worthy to take up my valuable time with him. She was the one at home worrying about where "her man" was resting his head. Besides, I was too busy being the "victim".

Without imposing on him, he allowed my right hand to rest on his chest. I didn't want to talk anymore; I wanted to make love to *my* man. I needed to feel like I was his one and only love. That I hadn't gone through my ordeal in vain – something good was going to come out of it. Plus, I knew it was nice and tight – glove fitting for him. Once I began to grip his stick with my bottom lips, it would be a wrap, literally.

I felt his hand begin to gently caress mine. My hand glided across his chest to his mound of muscle. I turned my body to the side and began to pull his tee-shirt up to his nicely rounded chest. Once I had it up far enough, I leaned forward to place my mouth on his small black beady nipple. My tongue worked over to the other nipple gently stimulating him. I used my free hand to completely unzip his pants to get them down. Not once did Kyron object to my touch. His facial expression was blank. I knew he had mixed feelings about making love to me, but he wanted this as bad as I did. I stood up and removed my shirt, bra and my boy-cut panties. I wanted him to see what he'd been missing out on. Standing, in my golden skin, firm and naked I began to massage my own body.

"Kyron, you didn't miss all of this?"

His body tilted forward halfway leveled to mine. His eyes communicated vibrantly, "yes!" I reached for both of his hands and allowed them to roam my body. My nipples were swollen and erect waiting for him to take one in his warm mouth. He was patiently exploring me like this was our first time together, holding my back tightly from his embrace. When he lightly let loose, he stood with me and he stepped out of his jeans leaving them scrunched up on the floor. I peered down watching him and seen that he was hardened for me. Instead of rushing our moment, he palmed my face opening my mouth with his.

"You damn right I missed this," he melodically voiced in between our kisses. "I missed the hell outta you. Why you hurt me like that, girl?"

My heart pace picked up. "Kyron, I didn't mean to--"

He began sucking my tongue, which prevented me from talking anymore. I felt so mellow, so relaxed with him. Hot liquids were forming on the inside of me. I pushed his chest to have him lay back on the bed.

To protect both of us, I stated, "Wait, you should use a condom."

He rejected it. "No, I want to feel all this hot butter."

To me, that wasn't the wisest choice. Yet, I climbed on him, raising my ass overtop of him and began stroking him with my hand. I let the tip of him feel my moisture and slowly eased down on him. I could hear him moan upon entering me. My back arched and my ass protruded out as I rode him pretending to be the Queen of Dick Ridin'. He regulated his strokes, timing each one perfectly. Brian McKnight was still singing One Last Cry, but this time I wasn't crying; I was moaning. I wanted this feeling to last a lifetime. I don't know why or where this came from because it was unlike me to talk trash. Usually, it was Kyron that did all the dirty talking. In my moment of control while I rode his back out of commission, when I needed to polarize this picture, I came out of my mouth and said, "Kyron, whose pussy is better?" His hands were squeezing my ass so hard it felt like I would have a permanent imprint on my buttocks.

"Serene's," he huffed winded.

"Say it louder!" I capitalized off of his humble moment. Then, I said seconds before he was about to let all of his frustrations out on me, "Tell me my pussy is better than Pumpkin's!" I could hear his breathing rhythm, but not hear his words. "Say fuck Pumpkin, it's about Serene." His fingers crippled on my ass and I could feel one of his fingers force inside of my ass. With one loud moan he exhaustedly let out, "It's always been about you, fuck Pumpkin!" My orgasmic rhythm tumultuously exploded with his, listening to him profoundly confess that. "My love will always be with you, Serene." He whispered before his body stopped jolting completely.

I closed my eyes and allowed the dark, but sparked filled picture of pleasure submerge me while tears rolled from the outside corner of my eyes.

My man was biz-ack!

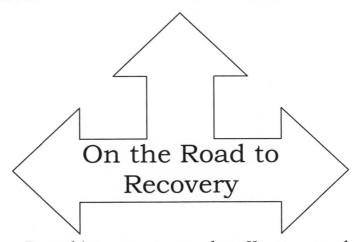

On the Road to Recovery

Pumpkin was up one when Kyron moved in with her, but I bet she was singing the tunes of, You Lost one, from Jay Z's *Kingdom Come* CD when Kyron told her he was getting back with me! And this is the story of a champion. Yes, love does conquer all!! Living in my mom's basement with no college degree or a new car and without stable employment (not to rub it in his face) and I had a baby on him, I'd snagged my man back. I'm sure it was highly influenced by JaQuill and his boy strong-arming me. And, Kyron felt somewhat responsible, but so what! I just won one!

It had been one full year of me going through the Kyron and Pumpkin stage and now it was over. Kyron and I were back. Later for that ho! I knew things would be different and we had to take it one step at a time to gain the trust back between us. I didn't expect it to change overnight and I knew there would be somber days. The main point was my man was back and we were about to get it poppin' again. I couldn't wait for him to put us back on top!

For the next six months, we were lovey-dovey spending quality time together, isolating everyone. We felt it was best if we were going to make it work. In fact, a few days before Valentine's Day both of us were feeling real got-damnit good and Kyron proposed to me.

"Serene, I know it's been rough the last year and a half and I want to put an end to that."

I thought for sure he was getting ready to give me that, "It's over", speech while we sat in a booth at Palodora an exquisite Italian restaurant. The place was filled with lovebirds and here he was about to damper their happy moment by making me act a damn fool.

"Besides all that we've done to each other," he emphasized, "I need you in my life. I've never loved a woman the way I love you. I know I fucked up in the past and so have you, but we made it through all of that."

That's when it hit me and I realized he was about to pop the question. But before he could do that, I had to make sure he understood I was a package deal. No matter what the circumstances surrounding it was.

"I've never loved a man the way I love you Kyron and if you're leading up to what I think you are... you have to love me..." I closed my eyes tightly and then opened them to give him direct eye contact as I spoke my peace. "...all of me and the things that come with me."

"I will. I'm not gon' say it won't be hard, but I'll work through it. I love you, Serene. I want you to be my wife."

"And I'd love to be your wife."

I leaned forward from the salad and placed an engaging kiss on his lips. I loved my man and the 2-carat ring that he put on my finger.

On February 14th, we were blissfully married at the Justice of the Peace. Yes, that's right, the Justice of the Peace and I couldn't have been happier. Scabby and Medina were our witnesses. I didn't need an elaborate wedding to commit to him. After all, love conquered all. There was a point when I thought about having a church wedding to rub it in Pumpkin's face, but that was the devil in me. The photo that would grace the newspaper was good enough. I'm sure she'd gotten wind of us getting married anyway. I'm certain he told her, and broke her heart when he did.

♥ ♥ ♥ ♥ ♥

We lasted about six months as a happily married couple before shit began to crumble. I was starting to think he just wanted to put a ring on my finger to lock me down. After the six months, we found bliss by way of getting high. We drank, popped pills, smoked good and then enjoyed each other's company along with passionate lovemaking. It seemed like that was the only way we could deal with each other. As much as I wanted him back in my life, I hadn't pictured it to be this way. However, it seemed to be the best way.

Stay Strong for Me

I heard the banging on the front door all the way down in the basement.

"Serenity, Medina is out there crying all hysterical and screaming for you, scaring the kids," Ella announced, as I rushed from the basement upstairs to see what was troubling my girl. The only time she stretched outlandishly was when Scabby was in trouble. I was certain this was one of those times. I flew outside to her, noticing her hair was all over her head – unusual for her. Her voice was so high-pitched that I could barely make out her explanation of why she was this way.

"Medina calm down, what is going on?"

"Wha... they... girl, Scabby got locked up!" She was acting like this was his first time going down and that was not nearly the case. The man had a revolving door to the jailhouse. Yet, she was performing like it was his first time ever.

"Where'd they hem him up?"

"They got him down the car wash. He confronted Jermaine about raping you and they got into it. Scabby was beatin' his ass when the police arrived. He tried to run, but they got him, Serenity!" she began crying again.

It was just my luck he had to be defending me and got arrested. "Damn! That's fucked up."

In a way I wanted to grin because I knew Jermaine got what he damn well deserved – an ass whoopin'. I was waiting for JaQuill to get his, too, but Kyron was moving like a snail responding to him.

"What did he have on him?"

Medina finally stood still and traced through her hair with her fingers. "He didn't have much. Maybe a blunt, a couple of pills, that's all. I'm sure he's getting charged with resisting arrest, petty drug charges and violation of probation though. He had six months left on his time. He'll have to do those six months on his violation."

Knowing all that, I don't know why Medina was that dramatic. She knew her man better than anybody; six months to Scabby was lightweight. She'd bidded with him for 3 years once, and then another 2 years without contact visits.

"Six months, Medina? You can do that with your eyes closed."

"I know that much, but it's the principle of it. Scabby is not just my man; he's my nigga! Without him shit crumbles under me. I don't know about you, but I needs my man!"

I deliberately stared in the other direction. "Marriage is not what I thought it would be." I wanted her true opinion on how she felt about it.

"What did you do already, hussy? Don't mess it up this time. Just make sure, you're sure you want him. Neither one of you need to string each other along. Is he still stepping out with Pumpkin?"

"Not that I know of. He said he left her alone when we got back together, so he says."

"Let me talk to him, I'll find out. Is he home now?"

"No, he got a letter to try back out for the semi-pro league. If you ask me, it's a waste of time, but it is a job. He's still holding onto his dreams of being an NFL cornerback."

"I know you gon' let him, too. At least he's not out here trying to hustle."

My face twisted up so fast and my neck snapped at her, "Why not? Shit, that's the easy way to come up. I don't see you complaining about Scabby."

"You may not see me argue with him in front of you, but we damn sure have our private discussions about it."

"Let's take a walk," I suggested. "First, let me get you a scarf to put around ya nappy head."

The way she came ranting and raving, brushing her hair escaped her.

"No, that's okay. We can stop by my crib. I'll fix myself up before we get going."

I knew I'd have to be Medina's support system while Scabby was incarcerated. She depended on him for everything. Not that she couldn't do for herself, but she realized the way to keep a man happy and pleased was to totally submit and allow him to be your King. I hadn't made it there yet; too stubborn and full of myself I guess. She'd been at that point. That's why they had a solid relationship. Although at this time, Medina was emotionally drained from crying. It was apparent from the visible puffiness around her eyes.

"We were just about to plan a trip to Vegas for some rest and relaxation," she spilled out her disappointment. "I told him not to fuck with Jermaine out in the open, but you know how Scabby is. He wanted to get at him for fuckin' with his little sister. Sometimes, I think he loves your troublesome ass too much. The opportunity presented itself and he took advantage of it. I bet Jermaine won't rape anybody else. Scabby stomped the life out of his dick. His shit probably won't ever operate again."

Silently I was hoping it didn't.

We approached her house and I waited outside for her until she spat, "Why are you sitting outside, come in stupid!"

I watched the kids skating and bicycling up and down the street. My mom never let my kids play in the front; they always had to play in the back because of the constant traffic coming through.

Urs was sitting on her front porch waiting to say something.

"I'm sorry to hear what happened to you Serenity. You know those niggas were dead wrong. Scabby should get JaQuill too!" she hollered up the street.

I threw my hand up to acknowledge her comment, but I wasn't thinking about yelling back to her a response.

"What don't her nosey ass know?" Medina asked me opening her door.

"She knows what she wants to know."

"You might as well get comfortable. We need to smoke to this." This was Medina's excuse on this day for getting high.

We had to smoke to any and everything that was good or bad in our lives. It was just another excuse to get high. I felt partially responsible and guilty that my boy got arrested behind me. Even awful that Medina had to bid six months with him so, I had to smoke to this!

"I feel so fucked up about this. Yeah, I'm glad he got at Jermaine, but the fact that he's gonna have to back up his probation is fuckin' me up."

"Girl please, he'd do it all over again if it meant him doing twelve months for ya funky ass. He loves you, girl."

I sat down on the living room sofa and reached for the remote that was sitting on top of a few Vibe magazines on the glass table. I grabbed the remote and the Vibe with Mary J. Blige on the front cover that was underneath it while Medina began rolling up.

"Lemme see who is up in this issue of Vibe."

"I read it already. You know C-Murder got a book out now."

"C-Murder, the rapper from No Limit? Are you sure?"

"It's in there, read about it. I think it's called Death Before Dishonor."

"Damn, 50 Cent, now C-Murder, who's next?"

Medina licked the vanilla flavored blunt and put it on the table to dry. "Everybody's writing books now. We are on the come up in all aspects of the entertainment industry. Even Snoop has a line of books coming out. You know Scabby got an autographed copy of C's book a week before it released."

"Medina stop fuckin' lying! When did Scabby get that connect? He ain't never told me no shit like that."

"He ain't gon' tell you everything. He knows your groupie ass would've been all up in the business try'na get with him, that's why."

"And he ain't never fuckin' lied. C-Murder would be my baby daddy if I'da known that." Both of us burst out in laughter even before we went through the stage of the giggles. I picked up the lighter and blazed the blunt.

"You are so stupid." Medina continued to laugh at my ignorance.

"No, I'm not. You mean to tell me if you ever had a chance to do a famous rapper, you wouldn't?" I waited for her to say no, so I could call her a lying ass. Every woman wants to fuck at least one famous man, whether he's a rapper, actor, or sports player and she's lying if she says she doesn't.

"Nah, not a rapper, but I will ride the hell out of Denzel Washington. That's my baby right there."

I coughed up smoke from laughing so hard. "Denzel is getting old."

"Age don't mean a damn thing, he's still the most handsome man with swag that I've ever seen."

"Well me, I gotta a couple I'd give the pussy to."

"Who? I bet they all thugged out."

I tapped the ashes from the blunt like I was smoking a cigarette. We had her house stankin' from the sticky green.

"You've got some nerve! Who is more thugged out than Scabby?"

"That's different," she smiled, "now tell me who."

"I ain't telling you," I smirked, passing off to her.

"Why not? You tell every damn thing else."

I said anything I could to collapse a miserable moment for Medina to make her smile and laugh.

"I'll give you a hint." I jumped up in the middle of the floor and began jumping up and down wildly. "I'm a thug girl! Uhhnnn," I began to rap.

"Girl, you don' really lost it, Master P? He's getting too old to be out there. Ain't his oldest son grown now? You had a better shot saying Lil' Romeo."

"P, may look a little tired, but he's still sexy. Those damn dreads, plats, whatever he got in his head needs to go though, if he wants to hit this here. Let me stop, 'fore his wife, Sonya, tries to get at me. I'm just jokin'. David Banner might be able to get it fo' real. He's single ain't he? Did you see him on HBO Def Poetry?"

"Uh huh. He is kinda cute with his special dark chocolate self."

"Yeah girl, he is. But you missed it! While he was trying to pay tribute to his hometown screamin' MISSISSIPPI, I could imagine him screamin' SERENITY as he came!"

"Girl, you are a damn fool! You know you wrong for that."

"T.I. might be able to get it too, with his little ass. I bet his dick is big though. Big things come in small packages!"

Medina laughed again.

I stopped acting silly and sat side-by-side with Medina to give her a side hug.

"Scabby's gonna be alright. You know that and besides, what are friends for? I'm here for you, like you're always there for me."

Content with the peace I offered, Medina responded, "I know. I love you, girl."

Scabby,

What up nucka? You know you got me out here feeling fucked up because you got a dude for me and ended up in the bing. How do you expect ya lil' sis to handle that stress? I hope you've been receiving the little bit of money I threw your way. I wanted to write you sooner, but I'm just getting around to it. Time is really passing. You've already done like four months, you'll be home in a blink. You know I miss having you around to give me solid advice. Its kinda bananas for me right now. Kyron got picked up again for the semi-pro team. He's making the same amount of money he was before. I mean, its decent money, but I want him to get a real good paying job or, well, I guess I shouldn't say this. Fuck it! I can talk to you. That petty ass check isn't enough. We need more – much more!

You know he got us a car. I don't even wanna make you laugh, but I will – a fuckin' old ass red square Datson 500 – talkin' 'bout, "Serenity, this is what we can afford." *Scabby you know how bad I wanted my man back, but not under these circumstances. I went through a lot and did a lot, but do you think I deserve to still be living in my mom's basement and driving a Datson? Times have changed. As a married couple, shouldn't we be advancing? I guess I shouldn't leak on you, you have enough problems of your own, but I can't help it. We can't even fit the two kids in the car if we wanted to take them somewhere because in the back seat the previous owner installed a big ass house speaker back there. I just wish Kyron would start selling again. Not for a long time, but just to get us on our feet. We need a crib of our own again and an updated car. Scabby, I'm telling you if he doesn't get his shit together, I'ma do the Beyonce and upgrade his ass! You know anybody? And one more thing while I'm venting, he's starting to use most of his money to get us high. No, before you ask, I'm not addicted. It's just I need to be high to deal with his insecurities. They are worst than they've ever been.*

P.S. I'm having Mejah Bookstore in Tristate Mall send you some books. You should get them soon. I also printed out and included Noire's online magazine. I know you'll love the naughty letters. Plus, Ree-Ree does have the scoop for ya ass.

I finished up my letter and placed a stamp on the envelope to put it in the mailbox. I knew he'd have a good old time in his cell with those naughty letters that Noire published in her magazine. Hell, they had me twitchin', feenin' for the future letters the following month.

Some people would say I gave up too much information, but I wasn't telling one damn lie about Kyron. We couldn't keep any savings for nothing. Every bit of his check was always gone and we didn't pay one damn bill. Now, either he was getting high, high, high, high without me, or he was holding out on his money. I was going to bother him about it, but lately his jealousy and insecurities were at a level I hadn't seen before. Probably motivated from the letter that Tomiere wrote stating he'd be at a halfway house in a couple of months. Which, I really didn't care at all. All I cared about was him taking care of Tashee.

When Kyron kept tripping, it caused me to examine the love that we shared. Was it truly real? Or, was it because neither one of us wanted another man or woman to cherish what we should already?

♥ ♥ ♥ ♥ ♥

I called myself resting, not going anywhere, and just waiting on my man to come home. I hadn't smoked or popped one pill all day and I was irritable. Kyron had been gone since 7 o'clock AM claiming that he had an away game: A game that wasn't on the schedule. I wasn't stupid, but I didn't want to jump down his throat with false accusations. It was after 2 o'clock in the morning when he came home knocking and stumbling over shit. He was high, drunk and smelling like it. I peeked out of the covers just enough to see him and covered myself back up not wanting to start arguing and questioning his whereabouts.

"The car broke down on I-95. I had to hitch-hike a ride home."

I heard him, but didn't believe that lame ass lie. Then again, the car was a piece of shit. It probably did break down, but his ass didn't hitchhike a ride home. He called somebody to pick him up.

"Serenity, did you hear me?" he asked, shaking my upper body.

"Yes, I heard you, but I'm try'na get some sleep." I turned on my stomach and put my head in the pillow.

"Why you fuckin' playing wit' me, Serenity?"

I felt his unruly presence standing over the bed.

"Kyron, you're drunk, go to bed." I could smell the liquor coming from his breath smelling like he had two 5^{ths} of cheap ass Mad Dog 20/20 Jubilee.

"That nigga wrote you and you hid his letter from me. You know I found it, right?"

That's when I was about to spazz. If he found it, he knew it wasn't anything to the half inked pages that Tomiere wrote.

"I didn't hide the letter; I put it up. If you read it you'd know it's not about nothing so, get over it!"

According to how Kyron felt, his actions in no way reflected him "getting over it". I spoke a little too fast and non-caring for him.

"Get ya monkey ass up! I need you to look at me," he demanded, deliberately wanting me to face him. I thought he was finally about to give me the smack that he promised.

I turned my head opposite of him getting real disrespectful.

"I'm not for this shit tonight! Leave me the fuck alone!"

When I turned toward this negro, I see him dumping a small white box full of dangling pink feet with round white bodies and whiskers – MICE – in the bed with me! Then, I heard him violently say, "I will fuckin' kill you this time, Serene. Don't fuck with me!"

I felt like I was caught in the matrix.

Petrified of mice, I screamed to the top of my lungs and began jumping all around the bed trying to avoid the mice touching my bare skin. Pictures were falling off the wall and my covers went flying over the television. The cup of kool-aid that was on my nightstand tumbled to the floor spilling on the throw rug.

"You are fuckin' crazy! Why would you do something like that?"

It had to be a dozen mice racing for shelter from us.

"The same fuckin' reason you would fuck Dabee and Lewis! The same day ya other baby daddy sent you a letter he sent me one too saying how much of a slut you are. Did you fuck them, huh? Did you fuck Lewis and Dabee? I don't even know why I'm asking a slut; of course you did. Damn, how many niggas did you fuck on me?"

My impaired judgment caused me to plead, "I've only been with six men in my life and two of them weren't voluntarily." I'd just admitted to him that I'd been with other men when he only thought I'd been with two. I could hear my mom storming to the basement steps.

"You two need to keep it down before you wake up the girls." She said her peace and went back upstairs. I knew she was coming down there to make sure I was okay and we weren't down there trying to kill one another.

"You trifling bitch! Why did we get married? All you want to do is ho. I married a fuckin' whore!"

It was pure pandemonium in our living quarters. Kyron was riddled in painstaking anger trying his best not to hit me by keeping an arms distance.

"Correction, I'm not a ho nor a whore. A ho is a woman that can count over 15-20 men that she's given it up to for free. A whore gets paid for her services. I'm neither. Since I've only been with six men in my life. That makes me damn near unblemished. My actions may have been a little ho-ish, but that's about it. Besides, look who's talking; your shit stinks too! I'm tired of you calling me out of my name and accusing me of shit. You are a jealous and insecure man. I told you before, if you couldn't handle taking me back you shouldn't have. I forgave you, you can't forgive me?"

No longer did I see the mice; they were hidden out of view. I stepped down from the bed ready for confrontation.

"You made me this way, Serenity. Damn, why'd you have to fuck two men from my team?"

I knew the truth hurt, but it was best to get it all out. "Kyron, it was a very long time ago. I swear I've been faithful to you since you've been home. I promised you I'd keep it tight and that's what I've been doing. You're gonna let Tomiere dictate your emotions about me? How stupid is that? If I wrote him a letter today and accepted his invite to visit, he'd rub that all in your face. He's mad because I cut him off. Do you really think he'll tell you anything good about me, hell no!"

"You should've never fucked with none of them and we wouldn't be discussing this shit now." He threw his hands in the air snatching the blanket off the TV. Soon as he did that, a mouse fled from its hiding place. "I've got to face both of those niggas at practice and games. And also face Tomiere's daughter every day reminding me of him because she is the spittin' image of that dude. How do you expect me not to flashback about what you did to me? I don't know if I can 100% forgive you. I know I said I could before we got married, but I was caught up in the moment. My feelings have changed. I don't know if I can do this with you. I'll always love you, but I don't know if I can fully accept that you let another man get to your heart. Even when you say he didn't."

A single tear fell from my eyelash. I wanted to yell out to him, "Fuck it, then! I can't do this either!" We were on the verge of killing one another. I had fucked up and so had he, but neither one of us could seem to get over it. We kept going back and forth about who did who wrong and how bad it hurt both of us.

"I'm not going to subject myself to this. Now, you're doing crazy shit like throwing mice on me when you know I'm scared of those damn rodents. Now they'll be living down here with us. You are losing your mind! And, I'm not even going there about Tashee. She's my flesh and blood and if you can't deal with it, get the fuck ta steppin', nigga!"

The air thrust pass my face so fast and I immediately felt the tightness of Kyron's hands around my neck trying to squeeze the life out of me. My eyes bulged out larger than they should; Kyron was shaking my neck irrationally trying to release all of his aggravation. I went into survival mode and deliberately plunged my neck down into his fingers as hard as I could. My mouth could reach just enough to bite the hell out of him to get him off of me.

"You bitch!" he yelled, holding onto the hand that I bit. I reached over to grab the small lamp on the nightstand and started thrusting it wildly.

"You wanna fuckin' kill me and I wanna fuckin' kill you!"

I didn't even hear my mom this time come racing down the basement.

"You two stop this nonsense! Have some respect for my house. Both of you need to get out of the basement. You don't pay me a cent for living here which I'm not complaining, but neither one of you take advantage by saving money to get another place of your own."

I was huffing trying to stabilize my rhythm of breathing. Kyron's forehead was dented with frustration with his adrenaline just as high as mine.

"My Lord both of you need to just say no to drugs. Your minds are all tainted. I thought you two made a wise choice by getting married, but as the violence increases between you two, I know it wasn't the right move to make. I try to stay out of your business for my on sanity yet, both of you keeps pulling me in it. Do your kids and me a favor, get it together and move into your own place. Kill each other there, not here where we have to witness it. And Serenity, if everybody keeps calling you a donkey; you better turn around and check your ass. Don't be a damn fool for no man. You can fool some of the people some of the time, but you can't fool yourself none of the time!"

The lack of warmth could be felt when we both caught a glimpse of the cold in my mom's eyes when she left us to finish trying to kill each other. Both of us stood silently between the catastrophes that we created. So, I began to pick up the things that were thrown about.

"I'm getting too old for this."

Instead of helping me, Kyron began pulling off his clothes to wash all his sins away. I didn't know how much longer we were going to make it under these conditions.

When he got out of the shower he lit a blunt disregarding what my mother requested. Sad, but true story, it wasn't until me and Kyron started getting twisted together that we were able to tolerate each other. When I was high, I understood him a little more. Even, often analyzing his feelings about how I dogged him when he was away. So, I smoked with him.

Just Listen

"Serenity, do you mind if we have a woman-to-woman conversation?" My mother asked me in the midst of the basement door and stairwell. She hadn't let me get out my first response before requesting something else. "Why don't you come up from the dungeon and meet me in the family room."

I was not up to hearing a speech about what happened last night if that's what she wanted to discuss. This was the type of bullshit you had to endure living under another person's roof. If Ella was about to lay on me the story about her and my dad once again, I sure didn't want to hear it. I had enough fuckin' trouble of my own than for her to relive her drama through my life. My man didn't want me. My other baby daddy destroyed that and I really wasn't ready to own up to none of the shit that I influenced. So, hell no, I didn't want her outlook of how my life should be handled. Life never seemed so bad when I was enjoying my freedom without anyone on my back telling me what the fuck to do! Now that it's all twisted, bombshells keep finding their way home with me.

I got my lazy ass up from getting entertained by Monique's Charm School on VH1. I thought I was bad, but those bitches are off the hook! I just knew my girl Saaphyri was gonna win – 54th & Crenshaw!

I was fully clothed in a pair of jeans and a white wife-beater that had an old airbrushed picture of me, Kyron and Dalya on it. That was created years ago at lil' airbrush spot in North Philly near Black & Nobel books on Broad & Erie Ave. I closed up my party bag mix that I was snacking on and laid it on the end table near the lamp before I went to see what she wanted.

"Damn, I don't smell anything cooking. You cooking tonight?" My mom watched my mouth move and volunteered her smart-ass remark.

"Don't you think it's about time that you start? I raised the one child I had. You have two kids that need to be fed. I can fix myself a sandwich and I'll be okay, but what about them? Maybe you need to think this through, not me. This is exactly the reason why I called you up here. These girls need you. If you'd slow down maybe you'd see that they do."

I fumbled with my thumbs like a guilty child that was put on the spot. "I guess that means you're not cooking?" I voiced ignorantly knowing perfectly well what point she was trying to get across. But why entertain that? Ella was bluffing; she knew damn well I loved my kids. However, the way that she was gawking at me for answering her like that, she may have thought different.

"Chile, I'm going to put this to you the best way I can." Her sternness with her raised nostrils let me know she was about to be very blunt with me. "You need to transform your entire existence."

If that wasn't a dis, I don't know what it was.

"What you mean 'my entire existence'?"

"That's the problem. You don't have a damn clue." She picked up a few of the girls coloring books spread out on the carpet in the family room that I should've been cleaning up. "You're a poor excuse for a mother. Please don't have any more children. I can't afford to raise another child of yours. You're making me old before my time. It's a crying shame that I have to attend grandmother's raising children support group meetings just to get some relief and to know that I'm not the only one raising grandchildren."

My mom was normally patient and lenient with me, but today she allowed her stress to get the best of her. The moisture on her face, nose and upper lip reflected from the sunlight. She never approved of my behavior when Kyron was away. In fact, once she told me, "Serenity, if you weren't my daughter, I wouldn't have anything to do with you. I don't like your ways. Bottom line, I love you, but I don't like you." So anytime I dropped off Dalya, she tightened up knowing I was up to no good.

"Ella, that's what grandmother's are for. I never asked you to raise Dalya or Tashee; you chose to do that. Now if they're getting to be a bit too much for you, lemme know. I'll still be living under your roof, so it won't make much difference. What you gon' do turn the kids away when they come running to you? 'Cause you know they will."

"No, I'm not you." She sharply darted her eyes at me. Her left hand covered her full lips purposely probably to stop her from saying anymore.

"Why don't you say what you really wanna to say?" Challenging her body posture, I stood there with my arms folded waiting on her to get into her gut to hear her true feelings. She acted like I told her she was 100% responsible for my kids. It's not like they didn't go to before and aftercare everyday while she was at work. Why was she stressin'?

"Get your damn life together! That's what I'm saying to you. Be more responsible, get a job, take care of your responsibilities and stop chasing behind men and the streets! It's nothing out there, but trouble. And, speaking of trouble, I'm tired of smelling that mess everyday through my vents. You don't even have enough respect to get high outside of the house."

I thought we did a good job covering the vents with towels when we smoked. I didn't have any defense to that.

"My bad; I'll take a look at that."

She unrelentingly tossed her head from side to side. "You just don't get it. You know you are just like your father, an irrational thinker and an impulsive reactor. Don't end up like him, sorry after the fact."

"Please, don't put my dad in this, Ella. It's because of you, I don't have a relationship with him now." This was yet another issue I could blame on her. "That's probably why I'm the way I am, so don't blame me!"

Very self-controlled she grabbed her keys off of the table. "It's my day off. Tell me why I need to pick up my grands when their mother is jobless? Speaking of which, when are you going back to work?"

"Well first, I don't have a car, you do. And, Kyron is trying to get the bucket repaired. I'll be more than happy to get them if you let me borrow your ride. Secondly, I'm going back to work when my job calls me back."

"It's almost been two years, honey. If they ain't called you back by now, you're fired! Don't you get that? And, I wish I would let you drive my car as destructive and careless as you can be. Not today! Look at your red eyes. Don't be so obvious with it. Visine works, you know."

"Hey mom, I still love you. Even when you don't' like my ways." I puckered my lips and blew a kiss to her. When she didn't receive that, I reached over and gave her a hug attempting to make amends with her.

Afterwards, I turned to walk into the kitchen to make me a couple of hot turkey ham and cheese sandwiches.

"Tell your husband he needs to buy a car that can transport his family around, not a two-seater. That's what you can do when he comes home from practice or wherever he is."

"I guess I can do that. I'll probably be gone when you come back though. If Kyron comes home before me, tell him I went out for awhile," I said to her, escaping away to prep my sandwiches before I put them in the frying pan. Then, I heard the door slam shut: that meant my mom was pissed with me. That's the only time she slammed doors in her house.

You Can't Teach an Old Dog New Tricks

Are women ever satisfied? Because I sure in hell wasn't. Contrary to what others perceived, Kyron was too overly protective of me. Scabby had responded to my letter and Kyron picked it apart.

"What the fuck did he mean when he said he'll always love you?"

"Are you talking about before he said 'like a sister'?" His insecurities were killing me. "Do you think I'm that scandalous that I would fuck my best friend's man? A dude that I call my brother?"

"I don't know about you ho's. Y'all will fuck anything with a dick that has money attached to it."

"Kyron, I'm your wife! Can you please stop calling me outta my name and names that don't apply to me?"

We were standing inside the car lot of a used car dealership searching for transportation that was in our budget. We had a $1,000 and our chances were slim to none for getting a half decent car. The white nicely dressed salesmen heard all of the degrading remarks that Kyron sent my way. His thin white pale lips were pressed together tightly. I imagine he was ready to get our money, get us in a vehicle and the hell off of the lot with us acting like two pure bred black folks.

"Here's the perfect vehicle for you," he said, pointing to an oversized dull grey Safari mini-van – no shine at all – with rusted spots above all the tires. "The mileage is low and it only had one owner. It is in decent shape, can hold up to 8 passengers and its only $1,500 with financing or $850 straight cash. Is that in your budget range? I'll tell you what..." he tilted his head a bit like he was trying to work out a better deal for us, "if you pay cash today, I'll throw in a pre-paid Boost Mobile phone with 1000 minutes. How's that? Everybody can use a free cell phone."

I couldn't believe that we were standing on this used car lot and Kyron was making this "Sanford & Son bucket" an option for us.

"Baby, you need a cell don't you?"

I grabbed Kyron's arm pleading with him, "Baby, are you serious? This is a piece of shit!"

"Yeah, and we need this piece of shit temporarily until we get back on our feet. Times are not like they were. Money doesn't come as easy."

"Do something about it; you're the one who wears the pants, not me."

"Get a fuckin' job and help out. That's when you can decide what choices to make. Right now you don't have any say so. It's whatever I say, goes. Now c'mon and let's test drive this GMC."

The salesman eagerly handed us the keys. I bet this was the first time someone ever test drove this van since it got on the lot.

"You may have to crank her up once or twice, but when this baby gets warm, she'll purr like a kitty-cat. Try her out!"

His non-skilled sales pitch made me want to pick up the gravel stones that were under my feet and pop 'em at his gray head.

"Would you buy this for you wife?" I asked him getting up in the rust mobile.

"I'd buy my wife want she deserves and I take it, so is your husband." I watched as he slyly winked in Kyron's direction.

Kyron laughed at his sense of humor and began to start the van. It didn't turn over the first time, but the second time the engine roared.

"Watch ya mouth, man," he continued laughing. "That's my wife you're talking to. We're taking this on the highway to test it out. If it rides okay, prepare the paperwork."

A fucking van! No way! I was screaming in my mind. The little Datson was even a notch above this piece of shit with a better stereo system. Too bad when Kyron had it worked on, it only cranked over once and after that it was done. That's why we were out vehicle shopping.

"We are sacrificing, Serene just until we get things back under control." He applied more pressure to the accelerator to give it more speed up the ramp to I-95.

Just as we united with the traffic, who was riding in the center lane? ... Pumpkin, in her spit-shined Impala. She almost sideswiped us with her car from not paying attention to the road, but to us. I could see her laughing and smacking the leg of the female passenger in her car to look at us. If there was ever a time I wanted to crawl up under a rock, this was one of those times. The bitch got a thrill seeing us down and out, probably saying to herself, *that's what Kyron deserves for leaving me for her.* Not once did Kyron direct his attention to her, ignoring her like he didn't see her, when I know he did.

"This is bullshit! I know you're not buying this van," I blurted, still offended.

"It rides good and we need the transportation."

"We need a lot of things. It don't mean we need this."

The interior scent was stale and it lacked cleaning. Kyron turned on the A/C to make sure it worked. Warm air and dust shot through the vents blasting all in our faces. I could feel as a thin layer of dust covered me.

"It's not blowing anything out but dust! I don't feel any cool air, only the dirt on my face."

"It probably just needs the compressor recharged. That's only $50/$60 dollars at the most, depending on who we get to charge it. That's minor." He checked out the heat and it was working fine. "The heat is good. We're buyin' this."

Why he felt it was absolutely necessary for us to purchase this van I don't know, but he did. We left that lot in the rusty, dusty, old-school-ass van as our means of transportation. This was not the perfect picture that I had for us.

My hunger for success matched my life at this time – unbalanced! Why couldn't Kyron just go back to hustling to pull us out of this rut? He'd better do something quick because I was getting impatient. I was beginning to think, *what's love got to do with it?*

Who Let The Dogs Out?

"Serenity, come the fuck on," Kyron hollered to me while I was in the bathroom applying lip liner to perfectly outline my lips.

"I'm coming, Kyron. Damn!" He was always rushing me when it came time for us to go partying.

Medina was throwing a welcome home party for Scabby down at the Longshoreman Hall. Everybody that knew crazy-ass Scabby was glad that he was home. He was always in and out of jail for selling drugs. Not this time though, he went down on a violation because of me and I still felt bad about that. That's why I looked out from time to time. Medina was faithful to this man to no end. She dealt with his other ho's by telling me, "Serenity, after all these years, I'm not giving up my man. We all make mistakes. Besides, I groomed his ass. I ain't lettin' another bitch reap the rewards." I didn't understand her logic of that until I busted Kyron's trifling-ass the first time he cheated on me.

"Come the fuck on!" Kyron pushed the door open. "What I tell you 'bout puttin' that pig shit on ya face in the first place?"

I took a second glance in the mirror ignoring his impatient ass, "Now, I'm ready. Let's go," I said.

Kyron had gotten so comfortable with Ella that he cussed and drank in front of her, but so did I. That's why I never said anything to him about it. She had become accustomed to our irresponsible behavior.

"Mom, we're gone," I hollered out to her to let her know we were out.

"You two be safe," Ella said, disgusted and worried about our safety. "Be careful on the road. You know how you two get when you get to drinking and drugging."

Kyron had on a long-ass, black tee with a pair of black jeans and Timbs on his feet.

"Are you going to take off your wave cap?" I asked him. It threw off the outfit to me.

"Are you going to take off that tight ass, ass huggin' skirt?" he replied, with edge trying to pinch an inch from my skirt.

"No."

"That's your answer then."

"I was just asking. Since you let your hair grow in, you should show off your braids. They tight. You should show them shits off. I took my time, this time." His shape up was perfect outlining his creative braid blend around his brown sugar complexion. At first I wasn't feeling the braid thing but they looked nice on him.

"You should take your time, every time. That's your fuckin' problem, when it comes to me, you're always rushing shit. You never have patience to wait for me."

Now, I knew an indirect comment when I heard one. I studied people's choice of words. His ass was mad about something else probably the fact that I told him he needed to find another way to get money. That meager semi-pro money wasn't much.

"Is this about earlier, Kyron? Man, you want to make money or what?" I instigated.

"Don't start that fuckin' shit, Serenity. I'm try'na have a good time tonight."

"What? You wanna live with my mom forever?" I was scared to ask because his family had lived as pack rats since I knew him. Their habits were pretty filthy. Five people living in a three-bedroom house was luxury to his common ass.

"Yo, you buggin'. I ain't sayin' that. This would be taking it to another level though."

"That's the point, Kyron." He seemed somewhat hesitant like he wasn't about getting money anymore. What I was asking him to do wasn't rocket scientist shit! Medina had informed me that Scabby was ready to get back in the swing of things. You know, back to his old tricks selling those bricks. He needed a partner to add to the money he had to cop. Kyron had the money from playing ball. It wasn't like he couldn't flip the money a few times to get us some more cash. He was acting like I told him to assist in murdering somebody.

"It's only a loan. Look at it this way we'll all come out on top. Scabby has everything in place."

Kyron frowned with the quickness. "How come you trust this nigga so much?" I picked up on his jitters.

"Oh, you're getting insecure about Scabby again? You've known him for years. Don't even try to run that bullshit on me about him. I had enough years of that. It's either you want to come up again, or you don't!" He was beginning to make this more than what it was and I had to give it to him bluntly. "I don't want to hurt your feelings," I began, but I really did. "Baby you are a has-been in the semi-pro league. The last time I checked, you weren't making NFL money," I said crushing his manhood. "If you really want to make some money you'd get down with this program. Not with a petty-ass football program that ain't taking you anywhere, but to play in the local park."

Kyron had this new way about him that I absolutely hated at times. Since he'd been locked up, he hated to take risks. I had to set off his alarm for him to move forward. We continued going back and forth until I finally lashed out.

"You know how it was when you came home from prison after you dissed us. Ella opened her doors for you when you left that tramp. She didn't have to let you move back in with us. We gave you shelter! I busted my ass out here for you working late nights trying to keep your commissary full the first year you were in jail and this is the thanks I get? Don't that amount to anything? Because of your jealousy, two niggas made me lay on my back for you!" As long as I could, I was gonna use that. Once again, I was thinking a bitch had to do what a bitch had to do.

Kyron's eyes started twitching, that's when I knew it was starting to sink in.

"Yeah, and you also had a baby on me while I was in there, too."

That didn't take me by surprise at all. He would often spit up on me his feelings about Tashee. We were still working on that issue. Deep down, nobody loved this man more than I did: even when I hated him, I loved him to death. I was his safe haven and here I was trying to convince him once more to get that money. His golden dream of being an NFL player – that was history and so was his money. Thanks to me, he had just enough money to flip a brick with Scabby.

"I guess you wanna end up like ya needy mom, living off of someone else, huh? You realize the corner niggas making more money than you, right? Don't you feel crazy? Remember how all the ho's used to be sweet on you? You could practically stick your dick in any of them that you gave a second look to. Now those same ho's ignoring you! Don't you wanna show them ho's that they wrote off the wrong man – a true nigga – a mothafuck'n true 'G'? I know you do, baby. Let's show them ho's and when the bitches come around this time, you treat 'em like the tramps they are! We'll show them together. You know you the man, daddy. You just have to step your game up, baby. Let me upgrade you."

Kyron would go to any length to please me and this would definitely prove it if he went along with the program. He'd spoke about his old hustling days after he did his three-year bid and said, "Serene, hustling is not an option for me anymore. I don't want nothin' to do wit' that life. That was my past." To me, that was clean and sober jail talk. I knew with a few motivational speeches, he'd change his mind.

"I feel you a little bit, Serene, but I don't want to give the system anymore time. You know how shady Scabby can be."

"*Shady*? Scabby ain't no different than the rest of these dudes you run with except those niggas broke as hell and Scabby playin' with some coins. So, stop actin' like they from different sides of the fence. You wanna get money or what?"

Kyron placed his key in the ignition with his keychain dangling from the steering column of the van.

"How come lately you verbally sucking Scabby's dick? *Scabby this, Scabby that.* I'm tired of you throwing up his fuckin' name."

I had to drill in him again, ignoring him getting territorial, with the fact that we were once on top, but now considered the bottom of the barrel. "Look at us, baby... people are getting a thrill out of seeing us ride in this bucket. I can't even fake like I'm cute as a passenger." I ran my fingers across the grey velvety fabric seat cover that we bought to cover up the visible rips in the two front leather seats.

Kyron turned the ignition only to hear the hesitation of the starter. It wasn't catching. After the third try, the van finally turned over.

"You sure we gonna make it to the party," I snapped being sarcastic.

"Serenity, anybody ever tell you, you talk too damn much?" I didn't want to push him over the edge. If I did, then he would show his bare ass once we got inside Scabby's party. So, I eased up off of him. I could tell the stress of our conversation was getting to him.

"Did you bring any other tapes besides Gerald?" Since we didn't have a C.D. player, we would record tapes at home from the stereo system. We kept the latest though. I had that new remixed B-Day and I wanted to blast *Upgrade You* so he could really get the drift of how I was feeling.

"The only other tape I have with me is Muzic Soulchild."

He fast-forwarded the tracks until he came upon *Teach Me How to Love*. This song had to mean so much to him the way he constantly played it. I let him dwell in his misery for a moment. Then, I tried to sweet talk him.

"You know that's my jam. Turn it up some more, daddy. ♫ *Teach me how to love, show me the way to your heart.* ♫ " I didn't want to hear it nor did I want to be taught. I was ready to give up on love's tired ass. It was becoming more painful than pleasurable. Kyron cut his eyes at me and let out a faint laugh. He knew I wasn't working with a full deck.

♫ *Teach me how to loovvee* ♫ I sang out loud with my trembling vocals in route to the party.

Party Over Here

"Don't park in the front," I snapped. "You know everybody gonna be out here. Park around the back, we can walk around to the front of the hall so people won't see what we're riding in."

"Serenity, people know what we drive. Stop frontin', actin' like we still got it." He always had to sour the moment reminding me that his boss-playing days were a thing in the past.

The feeling that came over me made me stop in my tracks and spit fire, which was very unladylike in my cute little girlie top and my skirt with my Steve Madden stilettos that Jaz, the shoeman, had replaced the heel for me numerous times to keep them looking nice. I felt my blood rush straight to my head.

"We still got it, nigga. Can't nobody take that away from us!" I didn't even want to get out the van since he insisted upon parking in the front any damn way, for everyone to see us. "Hand me the Hennessey underneath your seat, please." That was the least he could do after embarrassing me like he did by pulling up in the spotlight. Every damn car that pulled into the parking lot had its lights beamed on us.

"Here, take these shot bottles in, too. The bar can't get none of my money tonight," he fronted.

"What money?" I muttered.

Kyron paused as he watched me pop two zanies and gulp down a swallow of codeine, washing it down with two swigs of Henney.

"Damn baby, you try'na get lit ain't you?"

"This is not a game! With a life like mine, I need to stay lit. You either wit' it or not. Which is it gonna be Kyron?" I challenged, handing him two zanies, Ella's prescribed codeine and the Henney. "Join me in happiness. This is the only time we're at peace together."

"Let's get fucked up together then," he went along. "Just promise me that before the night is out, we don't crash this mothafuck'n party. You know how freaky yo' ass get when you get fucked up. You wanna sex anywhere and sometimes anybody," he slid in throwing me a kerm shot.

"Don't worry about me. I can hold my own. You betta watch your step though, 'cause I'll be on your ass tonight. I know that bitch is gonna be up in here." But tonight, I wasn't for her or Kyron's bullshit. I was going to show my natural butter pecan ass if they cut-up. I was in that kind of mood.

We must have sat in the car for at least fifteen minutes going back and forth about Pumpkin until Medina appeared.

"Y'all coming in or what? Or, did both of y'all come to play the parking lot? You know you can't be the King and Queen of the parking lot forever," she smiled.

I laughed at dizzy-ass Medina who looked like a million bucks was handed to her with her cute strapless dress, rounding out her big titties. She always knew how to coordinate her clothing and accessories.

"You look fabulous girl," I commented, giving her, her props. With all the females walking into the club, Medina was still the number one stunna of the night.

"You don't look bad yourself, hooker."

"Ssshh, you know my man can hear you."

"Bitch, please! Ya' man know all about your sleazy ass – you left evidence, remember?"

Now, Medina was my best friend and all, but that shit was unforgivable. Not only did she dis me, but also she sent a fire shot at Kyron, who was already vexed and Medina knew how sensitive that subject matter was since we gossiped about everything. She knew that he played my baby girl from a distance. No, I didn't like the fact it was like that, but I accepted it just because.

Kyron fell back a few steps and I could tell by the twitching of his right eye that the nigga was ready to bust a gun a couple of times to let out some of his anger and frustration. My buzz had started kicking in and by the time Medina and I reached the entrance door I was cursing that bitch out at her own damn shindig.

"What the fuck you mean, Medina? You know that's some straight bullshit!"

"Uh huh, bitch," she gritted. She was feeling it as well. I could tell from the Moët bottle she was holding which was half gone. "We better than that. This is not the place."

I cut in, "Why start it here then?" I had my arm leaned against the archway of the entrance.

Kyron pushed pass both of us because we were preventing others from going in. "Move the fuck out the way. Y'all are acting like some pure bitches."

"See Medina, you don' got his simple-ass started. You know it's gonna be drama in here tonight."

Both of us knew how stupefied Kyron could get.

"Fuck him girl." Medina waved him off like she wasn't the initiator of our little spat.

"Are you ready to get tor' up?" She held up the half empty bottle of Moét that I really wasn't fond of because of the bitter taste.

"Please, I'm already there."

"I mean get *really tor'* up," she emphasized. She acted as if no one else could hear or see her. I didn't want people to be all up in my business; however, Medina was open with hers. The bouncers at the door were shaking their heads.

We had already held up the door, bickering, causing a major disruption. People thought we were getting ready to get it on. We had too much of a sister type relationship to fist fight in public. We had thrown a couple of blows at each other before behind closed doors at her house, but that was it. We only fought like that when we both got drunk as hell and from all the bottles being passed and glasses being raised, with the loud music playing, we were getting ready to get pissy. It was plenty of sweaty, hot-breath, drunk ma'fuckas partying their asses off and I was ready to join the festivities.

♪*If you don't give a fuck – we don't give a fuck*♪, thumped as the bass rang in our ears from the loud speakers. Then I heard the DJ mix in, ♪ *Toot 'dat thang up mommy let it roll*♪. I went bananas in that bitch tossing my ass up and then rolling it down for a few moments.

"*Pop lock and drop it*," I sang. "Where my boy Scabby?" I yelled over the music, tipping in my stilettos. I wanted to welcome that bighead nigga home, *again.* Medina pointed over to the DJ's table where as many as fifteen to twenty dudes were showing love to him. Kyron was one of them. *Frontin' ass nigga*, I thought. Earlier, he didn't want to fuck with Scabby like that. Now, he was tapping beers with him.

"Let the men do their thang. You know Scabby gotta get caught up on the dirt. I got something else for us." Medina guided me in another direction. She always stayed tuned in on the high. It was already two rolled blunts in her hand and now she was pulling out her stash. "Here," she passed me a zannie pill and sat a bottle of codeine prescribed to someone I didn't know.

"Hold now, I just popped two zannies and had some codeine before I came in the party."

"Well, I guess you'll really be fucked up then." She pulled out a triple folded piece of aluminum foil, inside was white powder – cocaine. "Let's get twisted, ho! Take two sniffs, pass, and then hit that green monster (weed)."

"That's speedballing, girl! I ain't try'na die. Scabby know you fuckin' with this?" Cocaine was not my choice of drug.

"My man knows everything about me, okay? And, I'm not try'na die either. That ain't gonna stop me from sniffin' though." Medina was getting high like a general.

"Girl, I said I wanted to get high not meet my maker, hot damn!"

"You's a punk bitch, Serenity. I thought you were the truth. Don't be scared," she said taking a line of coke up her nose. "This is how we gon' do it."

"Scabby is gonna get 'chu! Forget it though. This is a welcome home party. Let's do it then, bitch. Put the high where your nose is, but I ain't putting mine there." I had fucked around with the wrong chick because after the second round (excluding the 2 pills) I was seeing triple doubles.

Medina was still getting blitzed when I walked off, searching and taking inventory of who was in the party. I could feel my eyelids hanging low and they were barely opening. I wanted to holla at my boy, Scabby, for a quick minute. The fellas had moved the party to the corner near the bathroom. My bladder was full so I handled both things. I did a pit stop to the bathroom before interrupting them. Scabby was talking mad shit about how he ran W-block in prison where inmates was getting money selling that nose candy. If I could smell envy, the room would be filled with stink because that's the feeling I got when I pranced pass the females going towards Scabby and them.

"Ma'fucka, I'm the nigga that kept ya girl from leaving yo' ass, sending her my signature handmade greeting cards," Scabby bragged.

I laughed because I remembered me asking Kyron if he learned to draw and write poetry too when he was in prison. Scabby said he was making a killing from creating soulful greeting cards. Medina didn't even have to send him commissary money once his business started taking off. See, this is the type of hustler he was. He sent money home to his woman; he didn't want to take from her by sending money in to him. I stood there for a minute until the fellas realized I was listening to them yap off. In a zombie state I went inside the bathroom. My bladder was so full it was about to bust. I opened the door to the bathroom stall, rushing to the toilet before I pissed on myself. Attempting to aim in the center of the commode, I was a little off. Piss began to hit the toilet seat splattering back on my ass. I looked down and urine was all over the seat and sprinkled on the floor. I had to hurry and get some paper towels to wash my ass and at least wipe the toilet seat.

I stepped out of the bathroom much lighter and relieved. When Scabby noticed it was me, his eyes widen with alert and so did Kyron's.

"There's my baby right there. What's up, sis? You know I appreciated those kites and the money orders when I first got down. You helped ya bro get a good start in that bitch."

I licked my lips slow, smiling, and higher than a mothafucka. I didn't even see Kyron when he raised his hand to yoke me up with his jealous ass.

"Bitch, you were sending money to another nigga? When you couldn't even hold it down for me?"

I was slow to speak and even slower trying to get his hands from around my neck.

"Yo! Halt that. Serenity is like my sister. We go way back. Matter of fact, she knew me before you locked that down. You know this, so ease up playboy. I'm not the nigga to be concerned about."

Kyron wouldn't let go of my neck and either I was too high and didn't realize he was choking me, or, I enjoyed the feeling because I was still smiling.

"Let her go, man," Scabby pressed, unbuttoning his dark gray button up shirt to his two-piece pant set, exposing his black tee-shirt underneath. I could feel it would be more drama if I hadn't spoke up.

"Scabby, it's cool," I managed to ease out with Kyron still giving me the screw face. I knew he was still uptight about Medina's comments, feeling that everybody called him a chump for marrying me after I did him dirty. "Kyron let me go, daddy." I was still so very calm and carefree. I wanted peace, not a lot of confusion. I liked to enjoy my high. "I only sent him about $100 while he was in there. That's all, baby. I was try'na look out for my big brother that's all."

Kyron finally loosed me and pushed me away from him.

"Well after that, I know ya sis can at least get a hug, Scabby. Shit, you got my man ready to beat my ass over you, nigga!" I joked as Scabby kept his eyes on Kyron.

The round of men from Rosegate started laughing and Kyron walked off. Scabby took three steps forward, greeting me with two wide-open arms to hug me. "I will bust that ma'fucka for you, Serenity. I know you're not still letting him beat ya ass from the past y'all been through," he whispered in my ear.

"He's stressed that's all. Just do me the favor and help get us back on our feet. We've been hurting out here since you've been down," I whispered back to him.

"Ai'iight, baby girl," he pulled back and kissed me on the cheek. "Yo, don't smoke or drink another ma'fuckin thing. You look toasted, sis."

I glanced over myself and noticed my skirt was still hiked up in the back. When I looked up, all the men were staring at my ass.

"No wonder y'all ain't move!" I flagged, pulling down my skirt.

Kyron came back to join them with another beer in his hand. "Go find some fish to entertain," he gritted on me.

I waved him off and walked back to chat with Medina and some other chicks. I needed to sit my ass down, but DJ Rated R started playing my shit, Purple Rain by one of my favorite rappers, Beanie Sigel.

♪ *Caution, do not mix with alcohol – it may cause drowsiness... the first time you sip it, you gon' get addicted*♪

I eased my way to the dance floor 'cause I'd been sipping Purple Rain all night. I was feeling this song in more ways than one. A warm body stepped behind me as I let my ass sway from side to side. His hips were in tune with mine. My

171

instinct was telling me to look to see if Kyron could see me, but the tingling between my legs was saying, "A stiff dick is hard to come by." And since, this man's dick was hard, I didn't want to make it get soft, so I popped my ass some more. I leaned my head back on him without knowing who it was. Instead of keeping his hands on my waistline, he began to get close to my Double D's. I found myself enjoying his touch too much. Soon as I began to partially turn around to face this man, before I could, I seen Medina coming my way in a fast hurry.

"C'mon, whore! You're about to get killed and Kyron got the rams too!"

"Wait! Wait!" I said as she wiggled me through the crowd. I wanted to see who was freaking me. I smiled when I saw it was Lewis, the semi-pro football player that played with the Diamond Backs. Lewis smiled back at me puckering his lips, motioning a kiss my way. Mmm mmm, I remembered how Lewis would give me dick for days. He knew how to treat the cat. "*Meow*," it was calling back to him.

"Medina girl, why you come get me. That's the boy Lewis I said that likes to eat pussy for breakfast, lunch and dinner." I turned back to Lewis and blew a kiss right back in his direction.

"Girl, I'ma hurt you! One of you bitches pull your handcuffs from your pocketbooks 'cause Serenity needs to be monitored."

"Oh, please do! Lock me up. You know I love that kinky shit," I teased back.

"Don't give her another thing. She is straight, okay! She's gonna have Kyron kill everybody up in here!" Medina warned her three friends standing around watching me.

"Medina, go get Lewis' number. That nigga got me creamin'," I said, glancing between my legs. I could feel the juice on my inner thigh from my moistness.

"No! That was years ago when you fucked him. Let that go, okay."

"Whatever! I need another drink. Which one of you ho's wanna walk me over there? C'mon, just follow me to the bar."

"No, you don't need anything else. Besides, don't you have a stash in your pocketbook?"

"Damn sure do!" I pulled out the Henney and swigged down as much as I could before Medina snatched it out my hand. Little droplets of Henney dripped between my breasts. I kindly released my tongue and licked the droplets off of them as Medina watched.

"Oh shit!" she hollered, "The nasty girl has arrived!"

We left that area and walked around watching the freaking going on. Lewis and Dabee were in the party. It was a wonder that Kyron didn't make me go home. I hadn't messed with any of them since Kyron was home. I never had any intimate feelings for them; it was basically sexual. With Tomiere, it was the sex and money that kept me coming back to him. He did take good care of this pussy when Kyron was down. Anytime this cat throbbed, he handled it. All three of them felt prided to hit Kyron's award winning trophy piece. I wasn't quick to give it up... just to those three. I helped build their egos by fuckin' with a woman like me. I was a top-notch pick. At one point, they were all under control and neither one of them was aware of my dealings with them. That was the beauty of it all until Tomiere caught me sneaking with Lewis when he and I were together. It was my stupidity to tell him I fucked Lewis and Dabee.

Kyron had his cake and was eating it, too. Well, so was I. You cheat – I cheat. The rule applied to us both. During those days, I had all of them dudes eating out the palm of my hands. However, after I had Tashee I was on the down side. Those same niggas started frontin' on me like I wasn't that chick anymore. Scabby was the only man that treated me like I was still a twenty-piece. All the others were treating me like a has-been. I had gained some weight and had a few stretch marks, but I was still stunning them. I was used to getting that one-on-one attention and Lewis was giving it to me tonight.

"Serenity, don't bug the fuck out," Medina cautioned, pulling me by my hand trying to cover my eyes.

"Stop it, Medina!" I was fighting her hands off of my eyes trying to see what she didn't want me to see.

"Uh huh, I can't let you see that."

I yanked her hand away and opened my eyes as wide as I could. My husband was on the dance floor with his fingers up Pumpkin's big bull face flirt-skirt, dipping his hand in and out of her stankness. Then, sliding his fingers in her mouth with no regard for me being here. As professional as she pretended to be, she was a whore for him.

"You are too high to start some shit. I'ma get her for you," Medina guaranteed me. I couldn't disagree with her more. I was too fucked up to try and fight Pumpkin. She'd mess around and beat my ass from the way I was feeling. I didn't even watch Medina check Pumpkin and Kyron. I was steaming, in search of Lewis. *Two can play that game,* I reckoned. Since my husband wanted to play mind games, I was going to play them too.

I went back to the spot Lewis and I danced hoping he wasn't on the dance floor, but in my vicinity. After I spotted him and gave him the nod, he followed behind me to the stairwell of the hall that led to the upstairs bar that was closed. The vacant stairwell was perfect for us to reacquaint. Soon as we got in there, Lewis started French kissing me with his full lips. His tongue was long, thick and moist as he jabbed it in and out of my mouth like he was longing to taste me. I pulled my arms from around his back and placed them around his neck. Lewis had huge broad football shoulders and a neck thick as a lion's head, but he was a big sexy linebacker and nasty, as he wanted to be.

"I know you're not wearing panties, you never do," he lusted, feeling all over me.

"They only get in the way. You know I stay ready. I know you wanna taste it, don't you?" With pre-moisture and all, I was going to let him eat until we got caught.

"Pull your skirt up. You know we don't have much time before your man comes looking for you." I pulled up my skirt quickly. Lewis lifted my ass up to his face and propped me against the wall smothering his mouth against my pulsating muscles. He had me moaning and gripping his muscle head making me damn near lose my balance. As soon as I came in his mouth, he put me down and pulled out his harden member.

"Do you have any condoms?" I asked looking down at his stiff dick, ready to go up in me.

"We never used them before," he answered gullibly, massaging himself to stay hard.

"Well, I'm on some new shit! If you don't have one, we ain't fuckin' – it's just that simple." I hated to let his good stiff one go to waste, but he needed a condom to go up in me. The one man that was getting it raw was my husband. If Tomiere would've worn a condom my shit would be still sweet with Kyron, but he didn't and I wasn't getting caught out there again like that.

"Serenity, please baby. I don't have any," he begged with his back against the wall and his dick dangling, hoping I'd give in.

"Too bad, Lewis," I said, pulling my skirt down. Lewis' lips were juiced up dripping of my essence. His soldier was at full attention and I wasn't budging. There wasn't any virtue in remaining fuck buddies with him. He had just played himself acting like a desperate pussy fiend. I didn't have any intentions on returning when I let the stairwell door close behind me. Since I was relieved and feeling avenged, I had to check on Kyron and that ho Pumpkin.

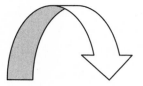

People Change

The next day I awoke with a horrible headache and hangover. I couldn't even maintain. That's why I stayed my ass in bed all day – until the next morning – it was now Sunday. Scabby's party was Friday night and I didn't know when or how we made it home. But one thing for sure, my body ached all over like I had been beaten. Kyron kept telling me to take a swig of Henney and it would put me back on my feet, but I didn't want another got-damn drink! I was sick just from the smell of liquor. I could hear the kids running upstairs in their steel tip church shoes waiting for Ella to take them to church, a place I needed to be repenting. Their running back and forth was frustrating me. Making my heartbeat pound inside my sweltering head.

"Kyron, please tell the kids to sit the fuck down!"

I heard him yell upstairs to Dalya to do as I said, but not to Tashee.

"I said to tell both of them," I repeated to make sure he knew, I knew, how petty he was being.

"I heard what the fuck you said, but Dalya is mines. Tell that other nigga to come straighten out his!"

I was not in the right mental or physical state for his pettiness. Shit can just get to you sometimes and that's where I was. I'd had enough of this bullshit.

"Look, we just need to let this go! I'm tired of saying the same damn thing to you about Tashee."

"Man, fuck you! You showed me last night the true you. I don't think this is gonna work any longer."

"Fine Kyron, you know what... it's always a dick better than yours."

"Yeah, and it's damn sure a pussy better than yours."

I tried to sit up to further argue with him, but my muscles were heavy, pulling me back down. I pulled the covers off of my nakedness only to surprise myself with fresh, red whelps all over my body.

What the fuck? I was hoping Kyron could enlighten me on what the hell happened to me.

"It's a damn shame that you don't remember," he said, stretched of his imagination, while I explored my body.

"Well, I don't. Would you mind sharing with me?"

"Nah, go find the dick that's better than mines to help you out with that information."

I knew he could see the exhaustion in my face. "Did you beat me?" I asked believing it was him. With me being drunk and high it was the perfect time to get me.

"My days of putting my hands on you are over."

"Oh yeah, when did it stop, the night before last?"

He began to trundle through one of the portable closets that we had our clothes in.

"Where are you going on a Sunday? The season is over, so you can't say you have practice or a game."

"Man, I'm just going out. What you need to do is figure out what happened to you. And why the fuck you kept begging me to go back on the block!"

"Do you have any pills?" According to the way he was acting, no. If he had, he would've been much calmer.

"If I did, I wouldn't give you any. You need to stop everything – smoking, drinking, poppin' pills and whatever else you doing. You don't know how to handle yourself when you're high."

I hesitated briefly before adding my comments. "I'll tell you what, when you stop, I'll stop!"

"Good, because I stopped yesterday. I'm glad you offered that. No more of anything, no pills, no weed, no drank, no codeine, nothing! Let's see how long you can 'just say no', he mimicked."

After I'd given it a quick thought, I wanted to rescind my offer, but I stuck with it.

"You act like I'm some addict. I can stop getting high whenever I want to."

"Yeah, that has yet to be seen. Soon as I jump in this water, I'm about to be out. Call Medina, too. She's been calling for you. I'm taking Dalya with me if they haven't left already for church." His eyes studied me. "If I were you, I'd get in the shower after me, you still smell like a liquor store."

In a distorted way he made me think I stank. I lifted up my underarms and man, *whew!* They were a little musky.

"Damn, you might be right about that." I wanted to delay his departure so I started trouble with him. "Kyron, how come you never handled JaQuill like you said you were?"

He rotated his neck around his shoulders to relax himself before answering. "I did deal with him. We had a man-to-man sit down."

"That's it?" *A man-to-man sit down? That wasn't handling him.* "You know I could've easily called the police on both of them. However, since Scabby handled Jermaine and you said you would handle JaQuill, I didn't report them. They could easily be down on a five-year bid for rape. They still have an open case, you know. I can easily close it."

He started that damn eye twitching and I knew he was getting angry. Still, I didn't care.

"I *said* I handled it. What the fuck else you want me to say? He's my blood! You know how close of a family we are. You voluntarily gave it up to Tomiere, why not JaQuill? At least he's family." His words easily flowed out of his mouth with his sick perceived scale of justice. I guess he thought *"ain't no fun if my cousin can't get none"* applied to our situation.

"You bastard! How bitter can you be? Wrong is wrong. How many times are you going to try me on the same damn crime? To me, I've been in the witness seat for two years and I'm ready to get the fuck out."

He must have realized how harsh his comments were because he came closer to me and hugged me.

"I'm sorry for that, Serene, but you hurt me. Sometimes I do and say shit that I don't mean to get back at you."

"You are so unfair, Kyron. It doesn't make sense. How can we ever move forward if we're always rewinding the tapes?"

I'd finally slowed him up. Instead of rushing to the shower, he sat down on the edge of our bed pursuing me now that I'd begun to talk sensibly.

"You're right. Why don't we start? Let's take the kids – nobody else – just me, you and the kids and go down to the beach to bond as a family. I know you agree that we need to spend time with them.

This Jeckle & Hyde mood swinging man had me going. I had to feel his forehead to make sure he didn't have a high tempered fever.

"Are you okay?" For him to do a 180-degree turn like that, something had to be wrong with him.

"Yeah, I'm straight. I'm just tired of living like this. I want a place of our own. Not an apartment, but a house. I want to raise my child... well, our children, not your mom and my mom. It's time we step up and do what we need to do for them. I'm not saying we need to dive into church, but we need to straighten up our act."

"You must be sick talkin' about church. I'm not ready to get saved. I still like to get my party on. Have a little sippy-sip, too."

He and I both chuckled, but then I got right back serious. "Man, my body aches. Damn, I guess this means you're not getting with Scabby on that look, huh?"

Kyron turned to face the mismatched curtains that hung from the basement windows.

"Hell no! I told you I'm not fuckin' around any more. You got me mixed up. I'm sitting hear telling you I'm ready to settle down and get right and all you can ask is if I'm getting back in the game? The answer remains the same, no!"

"It was only a suggestion, damn! What about us struggling? What's your solution to that?"

"Easy. Both of us need to get jobs. We can make it. I'm tired of playing in that bum-ass league. I can make more money working at the docks. My uncle is a Foreman down there and I know the Human Resources broad name, Tiffany. She's been telling me to come down there for the longest and she could get me in."

My radar went up. Of course it had to be a female that was looking out for him. If he knew that how come he hadn't tried to get with her sooner? He didn't really want a 9-5 to hold us down.

"How do you know this Tiffany?"

"Man, it doesn't matter. I just do."

"I bet. Probably somebody else you jumped off with."

"I'm not pointing the finger at you, so don't point it at me. How can we make it work if we keep going back and forth? Let's just look around and in today's paper to find jobs. We need to plan this right."

His sudden change put me in such a cavalier place. It wasn't a foreseeable future for me. Maybe for him, but definitely not me. He was up to something.

"Let's take one step at a time. You can apply at the docks since you have this 'inside' connection. We can take the kids to the beach on Tuesday. I'll work on not getting high and when we come back from the beach, I'll look for a job. Is that good enough?"

"It's a start." He kissed me on my lips and reminded me, "Make sure you get in the shower *soon.*"

My head was still pounding and my body cringed in pain.

"Before you get in the shower, please get me two Tylenol and a glass of water."

I watched him dip away to get the water from our small refrigerator underneath the stairwell. He came back with the Tylenol bottle and the bottled water.

"Drink plenty of water today to flush out your system."

"You sure changed from your first suggestion of me taking a swig of Henney. How'd you go from drinking to stop drinking that fast?"

"Serene, people change. It's not a matter of when or how, it just happens."

He almost had me believing that.

Despite the pain, I went upstairs after Kyron left and caught Ella before she proceeded to meet my daughters who were already in the car. I glanced out the window watching Kyron's mouth move in Dalya's direction. I figured he was telling her she was going with him.

"Mom, I hope you don't have anything planned for the girls on Tuesday because Kyron and I are taking them to the beach for a couple of days."

My mom was screaming, "Thank you, Jesus!" After I said we were taking the girls on a little trip. "He may not come when you want him, but He's always on time! God has answered my prayers." She stretched her arms open receiving God's blessing to her.

"Mom, it's not that serious. We're only taking them to the beach."

"Baby, God said if you take one step, He'll take two," she began to slap her hands together thinking she'd received a vision. "Get prepared to go to the next level however, as TD Jakes often says, 'New levels bring new devils!' You're taking a step forward. The enemy is going to do his best to bring you five steps back."

"Like I said, it's not that serious."

She didn't know I didn't really want to go down there with the kids if I didn't have to, but since Kyron had his mind made up, I was stuck!

"You don't think so, but it is to me. I've been waiting for 11 years for you to step up and you're finally seeing the light."

"If that's what you choose to believe, Ella. Anyway, have a good time in church and pray for us."

"I always do," she responded gleefully and went to get her car. "HALLELUJAH!" she praised.

Me on the other hand, I went back downstairs and drifted off to sleep.

Oh, about
the party

When I opened my eyes, I hadn't even realized two hours had gone by. Whew! I needed that rest. Sluggishly, I dragged my body off the bed and into the shower. After I cleansed my negligent ass, I dressed and headed to Medina's to chat with her and big-head Scabby. The sunlight hit my eyes soon as I walked out the front door. I liked to hit the ground from the sudden rush of blood racing to my brain.

Shit, I cursed closing my eyes shut to avoid the wicked sunray. I opened them again and began walking down the steps in front of my house. When I hit the last step, I could see a Nissan Titan coming my way. That damn Tomiere had been released to the halfway house! As if I needed some more extra shit to worry about. Obnoxiously, he's yelling out the driver's side window and he hadn't even reached my house yet.

"Yo, where's my daughter?" I was hoping people were minding there business on a spirited Sunday and not tuned into his ignorant ass, but Urs wasn't. I could see her eyes following Tomiere's truck waiting for it to stop.

"You know regardless how you wanna treat me, I will always be your daughter's mother, respect that if nothing else."

Tomiere oddly examined me to retain each unique facial feature that I had. He'd finally stopped the car directly in front of me. I wanted him to hurry up and get going before Kyron came back. Tomiere would've had a field day clowning us about our "new" ride.

"What happened to you? You busted!"

"Whatever!"

"Knowing you, you probably got in some shit. See, had I been wise like I am now, you wouldn't even be a broad that I hit. You're not the person I would choose now to have my first child. My idea of choosing a baby motha is completely different."

"And?" His weak indifference didn't offend me at all.

"Is Tashee home or is she with your mom as usual?"

"You guessed it, Sherlock. They're around the church. Go get her, but make sure she's home by six o'clock."

"Man, whatever," he barked showing signs that he was still upset with me. "You back wit' that nigga, ain't you?"

I flashed my ring at him. "I's married now, you know that." I roared in laughter.

"That man is a damn fool for marrying you. You'll never be faithful to any man; it's not in your nature."

"Tashee is at the church, Tomiere." I moved nimbly turning my back to him, heading to Medina's.

"I bet you're just as broke as you were when I snagged you up. Oh, and guess what? That little bit of jail time ain't do nothing for me, but stack my paper up from my businesses. I'm still paid and that nigga you got is still broke! You'll be calling me."

I stopped and turned back to him. I could see Urs all up in our conversation. "Not on your life! Just take care of your daughter, that's all you need to do and stop worrying about what me and the next man is doing."

My two-way beeped. It was Kyron hollering, "YO!" Embarrassed, I retrieved my cell from off the clip of my jeans.

"Damn, you back dating Boost Mobile, huh."

This time I couldn't even look at him and was happy when his tires finally screeched away.

"You up?" I heard Kyron ask. My spirit was back down, disgusted about my situation. Even though Tomiere's aim wasn't good, he still shed light on me. I was still broke and in a worse space than I was when I was with him. I wasn't hardly thinking that I should try to holla back at him, but Kyron needed to do something to help us get back... preferably hustle.

"Yeah, I'm up and on my way to Medina's. Where you at?" I could hear the slow music in the background everytime he two-wayed me back.

"I'm about to shoot a couple of hoops over the Westside."

"I thought I seen you take Dalya?"

"Nah, I let her stay with your mom. Somebody needs to hear a good word for us."

I knew his ass wasn't taking her anyway probably because he was up to no good. He wasn't even into basketball like that to dribble the ball, let alone, make a couple of baskets.

"I'll be home soon, alright?"

I hit him back one last time, "Mmm hmm." Kyron was just too sneaky for me. Recently, he had been disappearing or had some "important" place to go without me. I'd been deceitful, but he was carrying it to another level.

My body was still sore and I was dying to ask Medina what the hell happened before I blacked out at the party. Urs was now sitting on her steps rocking back and forth.

"Baby daddy trouble? Girl, you know how these men can be. All of them are jealous and possessive, but claim they don't want you."

Coming from her, I was somewhat baffled because I didn't even know she had a "baby daddy". Not once did I see kids coming out of her apartment just a bunch of addicts before and after a session.

"Urs, what you know about that?" I paused to have my occasional conversation with her. They say it's not about the messenger, but the message that's sent your way. So, I planned to hear her out.

"Girl, I have two sons that were taken by the state. Haven't seen either one of them in years," she said with ease like it didn't bother her.

I couldn't imagine my daughters being taken from me and not being able to see them again.

"Shut the hell up, Urs! How old are they and when did this happen?"

"They ran up in my crib when I lived in the projects. About 12 of us got busted. My sons were in there and as they locked us up, they took them out. The next time I seen them was in a court proceeding when they took them away from me. Byron is 13 and Mase is 11 now."

"You don't have any idea where they live?"

"I do, but until I get myself together, I'm not gonna disrupt their lives."

"That should be enough for you to get it right so you can get your kids back."

"That's easier said than done. I'm used to living my life the way I want to and if I get them back now the state is going to be all over my ass and in my business." She was still rocking back and forth moving her head from side to side watching who was coming in and out of the development. "I see you like to party, too. Honey, Friday night you put it down! You better slow up. You know that's how I started, alcohol, weed, pills and then cocaine."

"What you know about Friday night? You weren't even at the party."

"Well, you know I don't spread rumors, only the shit I can confirm."

"I heard that. But you ain't gotta worry about me. I'll never get like that, no disrespect."

"That's what we all say. I see Tomiere is still looking good. I hope he comes back through so I can blow him for a few rocks."

As repulsive as that sounded, so did I feel.

"You sucked him off before?" I quickly asked, getting scared to death of her answer because she was always straight up with you know matter if it offended you or not.

"Shut up, you know that's how most hustler's get down," she replied certainly, smacking her lips together. "Ask anyone of them if they ever let a smoker suck them off for a few rocks, bet 99% of them, if they tell you the truth, will say yeah."

I held my hand to my throat. "I hope to God that you used a condom with him and it better not had been when he and I were together."

She kept on rocking and smacking her lips. Her body language confirmed my answer. Now I was surely sick wit' Tomiere.

I walked up the block and it seemed like I'd walked a mile. I paced right up to the storm door and yelled through the screen over the music.

"Medina, come unlock the screen door!"

She came to the door startling the hell out of me with a black eye.

"What the hell happened to your eye?" I screamed. She stood there silently. "Well?"

"Bitch, I can't believe you gon' ask me that. Don't tell me you don't remember!"

I shut the door behind me and went to sit in the living room.

"Apparently, I did forget or I wouldn't be asking." Everybody was avoiding telling me about what I did Friday night.

She sat down and scooted to the edge of the couch like she was ready to leap at me.

"You opened your big ass mouth and told Scabby that I was sniffin' blow!"

My body tightened right up. "Yeah right, when?" I would never drop dime on my girl. There are just some things that women keep as secrets and this was one of them. I knew Scabby would get in her ass if he found out she was messing with powder. "I don't remember that. I wouldn't put you on blast."

Medina stood up in her rumpled clothing. "Yeah, I bet you remember this. Let me put it to you this way, I beat ya fuckin' ass for telling Scabby about the blow and I've been calling your house since then to apologize."

I yanked my neck back. "We were fighting?"

"Not exactly, Scabby punched the shit out of me and I beat the shit out of you afterwards. We tussled for a bit, but I got the best of you. Now, you either wanna rematch or to patch things up like we normally do, which is it?"

I didn't believe that.

"You need to stop playing so much. Where is my boy? He'll tell me the truth. Or, is the truth really, I dotted that eye!" I stood up getting ready to holler for Scabby.

"And you think I'd let you sit hear humbly, hell no! I would've jumped on your ass the moment you came inside my house. Ask Scabby, he'll be home in a short, but don't expect him to tell you a different story."

This almost separated us from being friends. I thought maybe she was engrossing the story to make me feel bad about getting so torn up.

"You took advantage of me when I was bad off? You're my girl, how could you of all people do that?"

She walked over to the stereo system in her family room to turn the music off.

"Let me tell you something, Mrs. Serenity Wells, you overstepped your boundaries. You know you and I go way back. Why would you, fucked up or not, tell my man about that?"

Now, I had to stand my ground.

"Correct me if I'm wrong, you told me you and Scabby held no secrets. I'm not justifying what I did because I don't even remember. I'm just saying that I thought he knew you tooted once in a while."

"You see this black eye? Does it look like he knew?"

The sophisticated ghetto princess was a bit bruised and swollen around her right eye. Judging from that, he didn't know. More importantly, I wanted to know when all of this abuse started.

"When did Scabby start hitting you?" I'd been around them for years and knew nothing about him abusing her. He shook her up a couple of times, although that was it (that I knew of).

"Please, you know he's no joke. He watches women like you and think all women act out when their man is not around."

Damn if she didn't put me out there on a cliff for me to jump. Why did she have to use me as the example?

"Huh? I don't believe that about him. He worships you and everything about you. It doesn't have anything to do with me and the way I behave at times."

"Honey, all men have insecurities, I just don't put my man out there like that."

"Medina," I slowly sounded. This did not take away from her *allegedly* beating me down, but it required more attention than that. "Scabby don't have no reason to believe you're not being true to him."

All this time I was thinking everything was straight between them. Of all women, Scabby didn't trust Medina! *The damn girl only had two men in her life. What hope did that give any woman?* I guess it doesn't matter the number of men you've been with, only the fact that you betrayed them. If he didn't trust her, why in the hell did he stay with her? These were the same uncertainties that Kyron and I were facing. How long do you stay in this stage though?

"I cheated on him before and he never forgave me for that."

"So what! He cheated on you more than enough times to pay you back. I don't understand how you can trust a man that doesn't trust you. As long as he thinks you're messing around on him, he's going to mess around on you. That's why I'm always skeptical about Kyron. He's too sneaky and I know he's out there doing something. I can feel it!"

"You and I are different, Serenity. I didn't up and have a baby on my man with a guy that he was doing business with. You ought to be happy that he took you back and then married you on top of that. Don't be so damn unappreciative. I know plenty men who would've came home and revenge fucked you and left it at that. That man wifed you!"

"No, he should be glad I took him back after he turned his back on me for Pumpkin."

"See, there you go. I don't give into that fantasy and those illusions of Scabby cheating. I don't let that drive my bus. It will have your fuckin' mind in shambles! Going fuckin' crazy, hallucinating, making up scenarios in your head, all that raggedy shit... you can't eat, you can't sleep, checkin' phone numbers, eavesdroppin' on calls, ridin' to places to check up on him, and callin' him off the hook to keep tabs on him. I've been there. I ain't gon' do that to myself again."

"Female intuition never lies."

"Maybe not for you, but I'll be damned if I'll go searching and snooping for clues. When my mom left town and left me her house, Scabby was the one footing all the bills, getting the house renovated and making sure home was straight. I was the one sitting back getting comfortable being spoiled, taking him for granted. And what did I do to repay him for his hardwork and commitment to me? I cheated with the next man! Do you know how that crushed him? Everyday, I'm sorry for doing that to him. I love him, you know. I've got a good man. Sometimes, you just have to deal with some shit to keep your good man. We all have flaws."

I understood her feelings. I'd stayed with psychotic ass Kyron after he dumped them nasty mice in the bed with me. I gazed out of her bay window until my gaze shifted to the front door. Scabby was on his way inside.

"What it do, baby?" His Timbs were clunking one foot after the other. I didn't know what to say to him or if I wanted to say anything at all. They were the ones always giving me advice. The counselor wasn't in me.

"No, tell me what it did on Friday night?"

"You were deliberately reckless Friday night and you weren't the only one," his eyes skimmed over to Medina. "She was too."

"Not as reckless as I see you were. Look like you stumbled into your woman." I couldn't keep my big mouth shut about it. If anybody could talk openly to him, it was me.

"Nah, she stumbled into me with a straw in her nose. You get down like that too? What were y'all doing when I was gone?"

In defense of Medina I didn't want her to feel that I put her out there like that, but she was the one who told me, I told Scabby about her.

"So, I wasn't the one that told you that?" Before he answered my frowned eyes deadlocked with Medina's.

"No, I caught her. You were too busy getting ya ass beat by Pumpkin with a leather belt."

"What!" I emerged from my seat. "Somebody needs to talk to me. Medina, I thought you said you and I got into a fight."

Scabby laughed. "She only told you that lie because while you were too fucked up to defend yourself, she was trying to get high."

Now this had me pissed and ready to throw blows.

"Please don't tell me everybody at the party seen us go at it." I was still on image time.

"Yeah, they did, but y'all didn't go at it. Pumpkin seriously got the best of you until I pulled her off of you and Medina commenced to whip her ass with that same belt she was beatin' you with."

"Where was Kyron?"

"That dude left you there. We ended up taking you home. I'm surprised y'all still together after that night. You know he left with old girl, right?"

"Scabby, trust me when I say I don't remember any of this. But back to you Medina, you told me you had my back. Why did you lie to me?"

"I lied to protect you. It was neglectful on my part for not looking after you, but I didn't know y'all were fighting until I seen Scabby run to help you. Be glad I fucked her up for you. You need to know when enough is enough. I couldn't baby-sit you when I could hardly handle myself."

"How much you wanna bet she'll never sniff a line again," Scabby stated strongly.

"It don't matter how much protection I need, somebody better be ready to bail me out of jail. They are still trying to play me. Medina, I'm not like you and no disrespect to you Scabby, but I'm not tolerating Kyron's bullshit! I don't have to. If he's gonna cheat; I'ma cheat! I guess we'll never be committed to one another." I let out a loud sigh. "This changes everything! No wonder Kyron wants me to change. Shit, he knows I'm about to act a fuckin' fool!"

"Yo, play it cool. If you react out of anger they'll see it coming. You gotta do it when they least expect it. I'm tired of this dude playing you, too. I told you, but you wouldn't listen when I asked you right before y'all little court ceremony. You said, 'I'm sure I want to marry him, Scabby. Quit asking me that question.' You said you were, so I left it at that and was happy for you, but after

Friday night, I know you two made a mistake. He played you all out in the open for you to see it."

He had me thinking it was more to the story and Medina wasn't denying any of the allegations he was throwing out.

"Well Damn! What else happened?"

"Pay attention to your man, that's all I'ma say. You have anything to add Medina?"

Any other time she was all-talkative, but now she wanted to be all temperamental.

"I don't know why you all quiet now! You got something to say, you need to say it."

It was that self-controlled behavior that Medina had around Scabby that I hated. I wanted to pick up the vase full of colored glossy glass rocks off of their table and bust her right upside her head with it I was so mad.

"Won't you light somethin', Scabby?"

"I'll smoke with you, but Medina ain't smokin', sniffin' or drinking shit; that's over for her."

"Damn, you sound just like Kyron. We must have had a hella night. He told me that this morning, but fuck what you heard; I need to get high right now."

"That's what got ya ass in trouble on Friday, bitch!" Medina stated sorely storming away from us mad because she couldn't puff, puff, pass.

While Scabby was rolling up, I decided I'd stick to my word and deal with my problems without influencing my thoughts through drugs.

"You know what Scabby, never mind. I'ma keep my word, and I would like for you to keep yours. How come you don't trust my girl? You know she is true to you. Yeah, she made a mistake, but so have you."

"As much as I try, I can't ever forget she let another man into my zone."

"So you sayin' it's okay for you to stick ya dick in another ho? And, you gonna try to hold that against her for the rest of your relationship? That's some bullshit!" This puzzled me and I prayed that he answered with his heart.

"Probably."

"That's so lame. Why don't you let her go then if you can't trust her?"

"And let the next man win? Hell nah! I'll make her ass suffer 'cause I know the minute I let her go, she'll go running to him or to the next man."

What kind of screwed up thinking was this?

"You know Medina ain't running to nobody, only after your funky ass if you let her go. You don't know how crazy you sound. You'd rather stay with an untrustworthy chick than to let her go, why is that?" I couldn't wait to hear his explanation of this.

"She fucked up, I know she loves me. That don't mean she won't try the water again, but I'd rather stay with a woman that I know loves me than a dame that I'm hittin' off that only wants the illusion of me. Medina wants the real me, that's why I won't leave."

"If that's not contradictory I don't know what is."

"You're a woman, you wouldn't understand. Ask your man. Let him explain why he came back to you. I can guarantee you this; you ain't the only woman he's laying his head down with. Not taking anything away from him, but he's a man with pride just like the rest of us. You bruised his ego and now he has to rebuild it. The problem is you won't be the only woman trying to help him get it up to where he needs it to be."

"In that case, why would he marry me then?"

"Serenity, like I said, he didn't want another man to win. Plus, if you have a little something going for yourself, it makes it easier to stay. That's why. He's in his comfort zone, his safety nest, but fo' real, fo' real. Girl, you must be doin' some hella tricks in the bedroom 'cause other than that, yo ass don't do shit, but get high and party," he laughed. "Honestly though, if he didn't still have feelings for you, it would be a done deal. He still has love for you that's why he locked it down."

I flipped it on him. "Why haven't you locked Medina down then?"

"Don't have to. Why buy the cow when I get the milk, eggs and coffee for free? I'm not ready for marriage. When I am, I'll let her know."

Scabby was in his "comfort zone" talking smack with his woman a few rooms away.

"You men are full of it. It's a damn shame." I got up to leave. "Oh, guess what, Tomiere is at the Plummer center."

"What's that mean?"

"Nothing. I'm through with him. All he can do for me is look out for his seed. You know I found out that he pays Urs with rocks for giving him head. That's nasty. He doesn't know what she has, and he's letting her go down on him?" I paused for a moment to see if Scabby made any sudden moves then asked him, "You never let her, did you?"

I saw his eyes dart in the direction that Medina was in and respond lowly, "What hustler in the Gate hasn't?"

"*Eeewww!* No, you didn't. You nasty, too!"

"She didn't start off that way; she wasn't always a crackhead. Anyhow, come back through if you need anything."

"Alright, but I doubt it."

I didn't want him to see my mouth watering for a puff of that heaven he was rolling. I couldn't smoke and get my mind right at the same time. I had too much investigating and confronting to do.

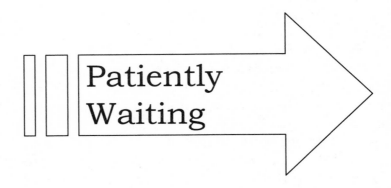

Patiently Waiting

My mother always said I was just like my father – impulsive – and I wanted to prove her wrong. Enduring the pain in my joints, I trotted home waving and greeting to everybody that was outside. I put up a front trying to show that Pumpkin didn't get the best of me. I wondered how many people seen me getting my ass beat. Good thing Medina got her for me. Still, I needed to pay her back. Looking over my arms and legs again I could see that the whelps came from a belt. I had it in my mind to kill Pumpkin and Kyron, but I wasn't cut out for jail. They were both going to get dealt with if they were still messing around. Medina talking about fantasies driving my bus, nah, Pumpkin drove my bus.

After all these years she still wouldn't fade! I had to find out if she was having an affair with my husband. He wasn't my boyfriend anymore; he was my husband – rules changed! A married man is definitely off limits in my book. Don't women know that? I would never jump off with a married man. That's asking for too much trouble.

Lewis didn't count. He wasn't married and all he did was snack on me. Wasn't no sticking involved!

I sat on the front porch not even thinking twice if my mom and kids were home thinking about how I could get Pumpkin back for humiliating me. I didn't see Ella's car, so I figured they were still around the church.

I knew where Pumpkin worked and I knew they worked seven days a week. I didn't want to go there and do something so petty as to key her car up, uh huh; I wanted her to lose her damn job! That would hurt more than a damn scratch and a few measly dollars for a paint job. I just had to figure out skillfully how to approach this. First, I needed a car.

I bet Kyron wasn't thinking about coming home anytime soon. He had to know by now I knew the truth about what happened at the party. I was annoyed with myself because if I hadn't been so messed up, I would've been able to control the situation better. No more drugs for me until I got myself together. They altered my thinking and impaired my judgment. I had to think clearly.

Boy, did I love the sound of the engine when my mom and Dalya pulled up; I wanted them out the car and in the house pronto. My daughter was so pretty and precious in her Sunday's best.

"Look mommy, I got my own bible!" Dalya flashed showing me her miniature bible. "They gave it to me in Sunday school."

"That's so nice, baby. Now you can read scriptures to your little sister."

I winked over to my mom to make her smile, and then hastily stated, "Mom, I need to borrow your car for about an hour. You know it has to be very important or I wouldn't ask you."

Her lips stuck out further than they needed to. "Where's your husband with the van?"

"He's not home and won't be home until later. C'mon Ella, I'm not gonna do anything crazy. Look into my eyes, they are clear, okay." I had to reassure her that I was sober.

"Did Tomiere tell you what time he'd bring Tashee home?"

"I told him six o'clock."

"I want to talk to you about that. When Pastor D is preaching and I'm trying to hear the Word, tell Tomiere to wait until church is over. It's just plain *rude* to have the usher interrupt the service so that he can come and get my grandbaby."

I held out my hand waiting (and hoping) for Ella to drop the keys in my hand. Hesitantly, she did.

"Okay, I'll be back."

I zoomed over to her dark mauve Altima to get on my mission. I was going to first check to see if Kyron was on the Westside playing ball like he said he was.

I hit the radio and all I heard was this loud static. It was on an AM gospel station. I switched it to FM radio and hit the random button to select the station. Michael Baisden's voice was nice and crisp. He didn't usually air on Sunday's. This was a special pre-taped show. I didn't normally listen to his show because he talked too damn much. I'd rather listen to satellite radio, but she didn't have it. His topic was cheating spouses – just want I needed to hear. It was interesting to know that I wasn't the only woman who felt that when a man cheats, so should you.

I drove slowly through the Westside, no sign of Kyron. For a nice day, I didn't see any familiar faces. Most of them playing ball were young boys. I knew damn well Kyron wasn't ballin' with them. I hit him on his two-way, but it was interrupted with a loud beeping signal. I didn't have enough minutes on my phone to call him. That beeping signal only meant two things: he had his phone off, or he was talking to someone else. I left the area in route to Pumpkin's job. If the bitch had any sense, when I got there, she'd handle herself professionally like she did when we were at the prison.

Pumpkin's job was about twenty minutes from the city limits. I knew the exact location because I'd applied for a job once before however, I never even received a call back for an interview. Not qualified, I guess. However, Pumpkin wasn't. She was this "big-time" professional making $40,000 or more a year.

Here I was so anxious and ready to start trouble entertaining that "fantasy" Medina warned me about. Contrary to what she thought, I believed different. My heart was telling me the music was off key in my marriage. It could've been my guilt of being underhanded and deceitful. Who's to say? I know I felt crazy high off this blood rush.

I zipped through the traffic and made it up to her job in less than 15 minutes. I tried to remain cool about it, but the way I was shaking let me know my impulsiveness was about to take over my emotions. My legs felt wobbly walking inside the building to the reception desk and I almost thought I wouldn't be able to carry out what I intended to.

"Yes, may I help you?" The jubilant red head, young, white girl greeted me with the visitor's sign-in book in front of her.

"Uh, I'm here to see Paris Henry." I'd almost forgotten Pumpkin's real name since we never called her that.

She scrolled down the employee chart to find Pumpkin's extension.

"Ma'am, I'm sorry, we don't have a Paris Henry."

I thought, *damn*! I knew this had to be her place of employment unless she took on a new job with another company that I knew nothing about.

The young lady scrolled up and down the list again, "Wait, we do have a Paris Wells. Is that who you mean?"

I felt my fingers grip tight onto the nicely dark painted wood desk to keep my balance and prevent me spreading out across the floor. I cleared my throat and could hardly stop my intense pant. I damn near fainted.

"Ye... yes, that's who I need to see." Now I knew on *this Sunday* it was a day I was sure to regret.

"Okay, let me give her a buzz. If you would sign in for me that would be great."

She handed me the visitor's book and I irrationally signed the name "Killa Kane". That was the first name that popped in my mind. I waited for her to guide me in the direction that I needed to go while she held the phone to her ear, steadily smiling at me.

"I'm sorry, Mrs. Wells is off today. Her message says she won't be in until tomorrow morning, sorry."

God must have known it was not the time, nor the place for me to catch her.

"Thank You."

My legs were shakier than they were coming inside of that building. How in the hell could she be using the name Wells if they weren't married or hadn't been married? I hit Kyron on his two-way again, but still wasn't able to get through. Those two were together! I knew they were and I was trying to catch them. Where could they be though? He wasn't dumb enough to chill at her house; he knew better than to do that.

I knew Kyron's favorite restaurant was Texas Steakhouse, so I planned on roaming the parking lot of the two that we had in our area. There was one not too far from Pumpkin's job. When I got there, my adrenaline was racing and I was blinded to anything else other than to find a white Impala and a Safari Van.

Please God let them be here! I demanded, welcoming the excitement. *Let me catch them in the act please!* I didn't really want to catch them because then I knew a choice had to be made. Would I stay with him or let him off easy with her? That would mean all of our years were in vain. Hell, he wasn't bringing home money and it wasn't like things had changed for the better. Maybe his version of "people change" meant, "change people".

Hitting the gas just enough to make it cruise, I searched the sidelines to see if I spotted their cars. People behind me were blowing their horns and all, but fuck 'em! I was in a crisis situation. It had to be over fifteen white cars in the lot making me go fanatic to see if the models were Impalas. I would be able to spot the beat-up sore thumb anywhere, not too many people still had those style vans.

Nothing! Neither one of them were there. *What if they rented a car?* My mind raced. I pulled up in an empty space and went inside of the steakhouse. I could hear the harmony of laughter mixed with metal hitting ceramic plates.

"How many?" The hostess welcomed me in.

"Uh, I'm waiting on someone. Let me use the bathroom and maybe then they'll be here," I fabricated a lie. I turned my back to her and kept on my mission. My chin was stuck so far in the air and my eyes danced around the room to see if they were hiding behind a booth. I was driving myself mad.

Unsatisfied, I went into the bathroom and splashed some water on my face.

Serenity, what are you doing to yourself? Everything you do in the dark comes to the light let Kyron's sneakiness. I deeply exhaled blowing some of the dripping water off my face. "Play it cool." I remembered Scabby saying, so I took my frantic deranged ass home.

When I arrived back home, the bucket was parked front and center. I got in the door. I was going to drill his ass.

"KYRON!"

No answer.

The bastard wasn't home.

✄ ✄ ✄ ✄ ✄

Later that night, the sound of Kyron's Timbs flopping down the stairs woke me up. I dozed off without realizing it. I glanced at the clock. This fool came strolling in after 10:30 pm; way after Tomiere had dropped off Tashee (Thanks God!).

Kyron was dragging and acting like he was exhausted.

"Where were you today?" I questioned, ready to straighten his ass out.

"Over my people's crib. Look, Serenity... I told you earlier where I was goin', so don't come at me wit' that dumb shit," he contended sitting on the bed.

It was like him to get all-defensive when he was wrong. I didn't even let him know, I knew, he wasn't over the Westside like he said he'd be.

"I'm about to take a shower and go to bed; I'm tired as hell. They worked me out on the court today. Those boys are still up on their game. That's why basketball ain't for me."

"Is that right?" I responded, mockingly listening to his lie. I bet Pumpkin pumped the hell out of him that's why he was so drained.

He lifted off the bed and his cell phone slipped out of his pants pocket. I gently placed the pillow over it so he wouldn't notice it. When he left to get in the shower, I jotted down every number in a hurry on a slip piece of paper. I tried to pay careful attention to the length of time he spent talking with them. I knew one of the numbers was Pumpkin's, I just knew it. I checked his text messages and there were two of them.

Where are you? Was the first one and the second was, *I'm ready*.

That steamed me! He was back cheating on me. Yet, he wanted us to become closer as a family. That was all bullshit to keep me pleased and not up under her ass. That's why he wanted me to get back to work – to free him up! He had seven messages that I wanted so badly to listen to, but I didn't know his code. I damn sure was going to do the Inspector Gadget and crack it!

I was sitting in the chaise chair when he got out the shower with water still trickling down his face. I could see why any woman wanted him. Kyron was one fine piece of specimen. I wanted to get up and kiss his suckable lips and make love to him. That's what my hormones were telling me to do. Instead, I got up like I wanted to dry his back off and slapped the fuck out of him!

"Why did you let that bitch get the best of me? Huh? What you still fuckin' her?"

How could I let that ride? He left me probably to tend to her that night. As a result of me smacking him, the towel dropped off of him exposing his soft member with his head poking out almost the size of his shriveled up balls.

"Any other time you're brick hard coming out the shower. Already had some pussy, didn't you?" I knew he had been shacked up in her house.

Unmoved and visibly agitated he spoke, "You better not put your hands on me again! Nobody told you to get all fucked up and start trouble with her. She wasn't thinking about you. You jumped on her and got what you deserved."

"Oh, you're taking up for her? Fuck you and that bitch! Y'all can have each other. I'm tired of going back and forth in this triangle. One year you want me; the next year you want her. Make up your mind!"

"If I wanted her, I'd be with her. Stop acting so childish about things. I'm here with you. You're my wife, not her."

This was the perfect time to bring up the "wife" issue.

"Is that so?" Why in the hell is she going by the last name "Wells" then?" If he had no prior knowledge about it he would've been as shocked as I was. I waited to see what his initial reaction would be.

Very calmly he went over to the dresser and pulled out a pair of his boxers. That gave me my answer... he already knew.

"You buggin', she ain't going by Wells. That's all in your mind."

"Kyron, stop lying to me and trying to make it seem like I'm making this up, because I'm not."

His lips shut me up with a kiss. He gripped me tightly and I could feel the moisture from his body on mine.

"Serene, I love you and only you. Fuck Pumpkin, okay! It's about you, me and the kids and we're gonna make this work." He wanted to convince himself more so than me because I didn't believe any of that bogus talk while he tried desperately to get his point across.

I did need his assurance to make me feel that he did still yearn for me, so I accepted his embrace. However, fresh in my mind, *was keep trying until you find out the password.*

"Are we? Or, is this just a damn game you're playing?"

"I'm not that dude to play games; I'm real with mines."

He opened his mouth and slide his warm tongue inside of mine, kissing me passionately. I received him and reciprocated the kiss. My hands went roaming all over his chest down to his torso area to find out how much he wanted me. I could feel the strength of him rise to the occasion. In mere minutes we were making love trying to convince one another that we were still meant for each other. He almost had me until after five got-damn minutes he nutted and couldn't get back hard! His cheatin' ass couldn't even keep his stamina up. I couldn't wait to break into his messages so I could bust his lyin', cheatin', no-good ass!

What kind of game are you playing?

The next day, routinely Kyron went about his business. While he was gone I called his cell from the house several times trying to figure out what the four-digit password was to access his messages.

I dressed and put on a cute little ass pair of jean shorts and a camisole top with a pair of high-cork shoes... my fuck 'em girl outfit. I kissed my daughters who were sitting in front of the television watching cartoons. We only had one more day until we journeyed to the beach. I didn't know if I'd last that long before I blew my cover of investigating.

As if I didn't have anything better to do, I went over to bother Medina and Scabby and to vent out my problems to them. Scabby was on the porch chatting it up with some guys that I hadn't seen before. I guessed they were his new business partners.

"Keep right on going inside the house," he said to me catching me staring at his new associates. I was just checking them out, that's all, no harm done. "That's my lil' sister man, and she's married," he blurted out to them in case they were going to ask who I was.

I welcomed myself to the kitchen where I found Medina was cooking a late breakfast.

"Hook a sista up. Let me hold a piece of that scrapple in my mouth."

The pan was crackling from the scrapple cooking.

"Can you get your nose back please? I'm try'na cook me and my man something to eat."

I took a seat on one of the two bar stools, just passing time with her.

"Girl, you can let me get a sandwich. Don't be stingy with food. Anyway, who's that on the porch with Scabby?"

"Don't even worry about it. You have enough problems."

"And that I do. I'm trying to figure out Kyron's password to his phone so I can bust his ass wide open."

"There you go asking for trouble."

"No I'm not. I have my reasons. I'm taking suggestions if you're offering. Can you help me?"

Medina paused for a moment.

"I figured Scabby's out once and when I did, it caused me extreme chaos in my life."

"That's because you stayed with him after you found out he cheated, Medina. If I find out that Kyron is cheating on me again, I'm not staying with him. That's my word!"

"Mmm hmm. Let me think. Did you try his birthday?"

"Yep."

"His last four digits of his social security number?"

"Did that."

"What about the last four digits of his cell?"

"Girl, now you know he's been changed that."

"Yeah, you're right about that, who doesn't? Damn, what else could it be? Did you try your daughter's birthday?"

"You're on to something now, girl. Where's the phone?"

I looked over on the kitchen wall where the receiver was without the phone. I hit the alert button to follow the sound. I chased the signal to the porch. Scabby had it out there with him. I didn't want to interrupt them or seem like I was pressed trying to get their attention.

"Lemme get the cordless, Scabby." I partially leaned out the front door and extended my hand for him to give me the phone.

"Whazzup, Serenity? Wit' ya sexy ass." I heard one of the guys on the porch ask me. I glanced up to him, giving him a once over. He was cute and dressed nice, nothing extravagant – a short sleeve Michael Vick Atlanta Falcons red/white/black football jersey with a pair of capris (for men) on. Scabby placed the phone in my hand and pushed me back inside.

"Here girl," he said and turned to the guy and said, "Hey Skeet, my sister is off limits. I told you, she's married."

I took the phone and watched how Skeet ignored Scabby by winking at me anyway.

Men, I laughed to myself and began to try my chances of getting into Kyron's voicemail.

I could smell buttermilk pancakes in addition to the scrapple. Medina was hooking it up! My stomach was growling, but my hunger to find out who was leaving Kyron messages was worse.

"Okay, Medina! Here I go."

"Wait!" she yelled, running out the kitchen and I stopped dialing. "Are you sure you wanna go this far? You know if you find out he's messing around you're gonna go off. Maybe even kill the man."

I felt like I was back in high school again defending my "girlfriend status".

"I doubt that. Anyway, I've come too far to turn back now. Besides, this may not even be the password," I speculated.

"Suppose it is?" she stressed.

"Then, I get what I set out to accomplish."

"You have all the answers. Try it then."

She sounded just like my damn mom saying that. The palms on my hands were getting moist and my fingers began to shake. I dialed the number slowly pushing one number at a time to make sure I was dialing the numbers correctly. The phone began ringing.

Kyron answered!

"Talk fast because I'm in the middle of a very important conversation," he said rushing me off the phone before I could even say anything.

Important conversation my ass! It could've been Medina or Scabby calling him from their number.

"What did you answer the phone for if you were so damn busy?"

I know he felt the tension in my tone. That's why he responded; "I'll see you when I get home. I'll be there shortly."

I was glad he hung up because I knew the next time I called he'd let it go straight to voicemail like I needed it to.

"Maybe it's not meant for you to find out," Medina stated, standing by my side with a full plate of breakfast in her hand to deliver to Scabby. Ghetto fabulous didn't have any problem eating outside on the porch.

"You forgot the syrup. Wonder about that!" I stared down at the cordless and dialed Kyron's number again. This time it went straight to voicemail. I hit the pound key and tried my luck keying in Dalya's birth date when I was prompted to enter the password.

Invalid password, the automated voice recording sounded.

"Aaaaggghhh," I screamed out getting angrier and angrier.

Medina walked back into the room.

"What happened?"

"Invalid password." With frustration I imitated the automated recording.

"I guess it's not meant for you to find out."

"Shut up Medina! I don't feel like hearing that."

I wanted to throw their phone across the room. Then, it dawned on me to check the year

Kyron was born. I went through the entire process again. I pressed 1981, when I was prompted to enter the password.

You have three messages! The voice recording pleasantly alarmed in my ears.

Bingo! I'd done it. I rapidly pressed (1) for the messages.

"Medina, I cracked it!"

I saw her shaking and nodding her head. "I hope it's not what it seems."

First message: *Hey bay, I've been hitting your phone all day, why are you ignoring me? Call me when you get this.*

That voice didn't sound familiar to me. It wasn't Pumpkin. He had somebody else! I was eager to hear the second message to see if this same person would leave their name, but the second message was just a hang up. I hit the pound button to retrieve the last message. That's when my blood pressure shot up sky-high.

Hey baby, I hope you can get free sometime today to come see your precious daughters and me. They miss you as much as I do. All of these years that we've been together, even though it was off and on, my heart has always been with you. You were my first and will remain my last. I mean that. I've always been there for you and always will, no matter how much love you have in your heart for Serenity. I know she's your first love, but through the years she's changed. You're chasing a love that has gone astray. I would never betray you by having another man's child. You know with me, it's never been about the money or the respect you had in the streets. Baby, I am the woman that upgraded you; Serenity has you riding cheap in a run down cargo van. I'd never let you go out like that. You know with me it's solely based on the love we share and our daughters together. I've always had my own. Instead of creating a hardship on you, I've been your backbone. Yes, I was devastated that you would marry her after she had a baby on you. Yet, I still played my position. I even told you that I'd be a witness to your marriage if you needed me to be. That's how I ride for you! I'd rather be #2 in your life than to be out of it completely. That's why with your approval and in honor of you, I changed my last name. One day I hope to become your wife to make our family valid. The door is always open for you – use your key. I'll be waiting...

My body was a bundle of nerves, worse than the shivers from being cold. I dropped the cordless, busting off the back cover that protected the battery. The noise of the phone rumbled through the kitchen.

"What is it Serenity!" Medina came rushing towards me from my reaction. Her right hand gently touched my shoulder. I knew she could see the displeasure in my eyes.

"He's got another family! Pumpkin's two foster sisters aren't her sisters; they're really Kyron's daughters!"

The room was spinning around me and I could hear voices outside: although, they appeared to be right in front of me.

"I told you not to look for trouble. Wow. Do you believe her? What you gon' do?" Medina bent down to pick up the back piece of the phone that darted across the floor.

"That hatin' ass bitch ain't lying. Yeah, I believe her. She's stupid enough to hide her kids to protect him just to be with him. I'm leaving him, that's what I'm gon' do. I'm not going through this bullshit. I hate him for what he's done to me! He's a liar and a cheater! A no-good bastard!"

"And, not any different than you. He's forgiven you, can't you forgive him?"

Medina was trying hard to secure the back piece of the cordless when I smacked it out of her hand.

"What the fuck are you saying?" He's been cheating on me for years! We got married and this man knew he had babies on me, too!"

I could hear the screen door shut and Scabby's footsteps.

"Yo, what's up wit' you? I could hear you outside screamin' and whatnot."

"He got me back, Scabby. Kyron has two kids by Pumpkin and they're still messing around. She even changed her last name to Wells."

I wanted him to embrace me and allow me to cry on his shoulders, but it didn't happen that way. Scabby wanted me to take the strong way out.

"So, fuck him. Move on and leave him. The nigga ain't about makin' paper no more anyway. Let that bamma bitch have him. You wanted a way out, didn't you?"

"What about all that I've gone through?" My eyes moved from his to Medina's in search of a righteous response. "We're supposed to take the kids to the beach tomorrow."

"Don't do anything out of the ordinary tonight. Act like everything is kosher and go along with the plans." Scabby began shaking his head in disbelief. "You never listen. I told you, get 'im first before he gets you. Whatever you do, don't drag your kids in this. Leave them home."

"But I promised them and they are looking forward to it. Besides, they will help me remain calm."

"That's bullshit!" Medina spat. "You know damn well they won't make a difference. I say cancel the trip all together. You don't want them in the middle of you and Kyron's mess."

"No, don't cancel it. You go, but don't take the kids," Scabby interjected.

Both of them weren't getting it. The children were the focal point of the trip. If they didn't go, Kyron probably wouldn't go and I needed him there so I could confront him.

"Spark somethin'," I suggested in the middle of them going back and forth with what I should do. "If you have pills, let me get a couple of them too," I asked of Scabby.

He dug into his pocket and pulled out a clear plastic baggie of pills removing two white pills and handed them to me.

"These will calm and relax you."

I admired Medina for disassociating herself when drugs were involved now. I wondered if it was only because of Scabby's influence that she left everything alone or, if the temptation was too strong for her to be in our presence. 'Cause, she quickly left the room when the pills exchanged hands.

"Thank you, boo. I can't go home in this state or I'll end up getting a charge."

We followed behind Medina and moved our conversation to the living room. I'd gone against my word by poppin' pills and smokin' weed when Scabby began to spark. Now, I was beginning to think that I did have a slight problem: A problem of not being able to resolve conflict in my life without getting high. Still, I savored my calmness and peaceful moment nodding off into a deep sleep on their couch.

It was after 6 o'clock the next morning when I woke up, fully clothed on Medina and Scabby's couch. Whatever Scabby gave me knocked me the hell out. Normally, I'd dream, although this time, nothing but stillness. I didn't want to bother them so I left out quietly. I questioned myself whether Kyron had called around looking for me since I'd been out all night 'cause he sure in hell didn't come looking for me at their house.

The streets in our neighborhood were quiet and absent of people, except me. I opened my mouth to yawn and smelled the awful scent of my own morning breath. I took my time walking home. Many negative thoughts crowded and raced through my mind. As soon as I reached the steps, I saw the front door opening. Kyron was standing front and center, shirtless, with a pair of basketball shorts on waiting for me to come inside fronting like he was heated. I reminded myself to stay civil and not bug out to avoid being reactive.

"You're not gonna mess this up for Dalya, nor Tashee. They were talking about this all yesterday. We are still gonna take them like we promised."

I remained silent.

"Look at you; you look like you've been getting high all night long. Where were you? I called everywhere for you."

My feet slowly dragged towards the basement while my mouth remained silent.

"Get your shit together because we're leaving at 8 o'clock. We can talk about you later."

It amazed me how Kyron was putting up this front like he was really a family man. When he was nothing more than a perpetrator. I gathered my belongings and put them in a duffle bag. Afterwards, I took a shower, brushed my teeth and manned my hair. I kept taking short exhalations to stabilize my anxiousness.

Dressed and ready, I went upstairs to see if my mom had gotten the girls up to get showered and dressed. It was close to 7:30 and I wasn't quite prepared to sit in our van that didn't have a/c and it was going to be a record high temperature day per the news forecast that I heard from the loud television in the family room. That's the sole reason we had to get going early. I had administered extra deodorant and I hoped that the Secret pear scent would work overtime. I was doing a great job playing it cool, possibly because I was still somewhat drowsy. I knew when I became fully alert the situation was going to turn ugly.

My mom was giving out hugs and kisses to my daughters as they made their way toward the front door. Both of them were prepared for the beach wearing their two-piece bathing suits.

"You two take care of mommy and daddy, okay."

"I'll keep them straight mom-mom," Dayla innocently stated and gave Ella one last hug.

"Take care of my grands," my mom said staring over Dalya's shoulders to me.

"Of course. Come on Dayla and Tashee. Grab your bags and let's hit it."

Soon as we got out front, I see Kyron and Tomiere exchanging words. It wasn't loud and confrontational, but both mouths were moving. Both of them were maintaining their personal space.

"Daddy!" Tashee went sprinting over to Tomiere.

Soon as both of them seen her approaching, they became silent.

"Dalya, get in the van." I didn't want her too close in case something jumped off.

I went to both of them hoping to defuse a negative situation. Tashee received her dad lovingly and I could see Kyron's eye begin twitching.

"That's enough now. Tashee go get in the car with your sister."

"Alright, mom. Dad, I'll call you when we get back."

"You do that princess," Tomiere beamed, giving her a firm loving hug.

Tashee ran back to the car leaving the three of us alone. I waited to see which one of them was going to continue exchanging words. However, neither one of them did. So, I took the initiative.

"Tomiere, Tashee won't be home for a couple of days. We're going to the beach."

Kyron immediately jumped in yelling, "You don't have to tell him where the fuck we're going. It's none of his damn business!"

Here went the domino effect. Tomiere began getting ignorant about it as well.

"Fuck you mean, it ain't none of my business? Anytime Tashee is involved it's **my business**. And nobody is going to come between that."

Tomiere was plainly ready to start some shit. Both of them had unresolved issues. If I hadn't stepped in, my daughters would etch this day in their memory forever.

"Be men about this. Tomiere, Tashee will see you when she gets back."

He wasn't trying to hear anything I had to say.

"Next time you need to let me know when my daughter is leaving. I had plans for us today. Don't me make me take ya ass to Family Court for visitation rights."

"Whatever, Tomiere! You won't have to fight me; you'll have to fight Ella."

My head ached so badly and I had a troubled spirit.

"Kyron, are you ready to go?" It was absolutely killing me not to get ig-nant with both of them.

Kyron turned towards the van and I followed until I heard Urs call for me.

"Serenity, com'ere for a minute. I got something to tell you."

I walked over to her and took notes on the details she dished.

When I came back and neared the van I heard Tomiere yell out, "That's a real nice ride y'all got."

I wasn't for his sarcasm so I ignored his ignorant laughter.

"Let's ride," Kyron suggested still teed-off, gathering the grocery bags filled with chicken and sandwiches that Ella had packed. He was doing a helluva job acting like his shit didn't stink.

The girls had packed ride games to entertain themselves along the way. This was the first time I felt family-oriented and it was fake. I didn't feel bad that I would be the cause that would ultimately ruin this little bond.

Kyron ain't shit! I thought, watching him gather up his tapes. Each and every second, I was fighting back my irate-filled thoughts.

"You ready?" he asked me.

"As I'm gonna be," I responded, biting my bottom lip to keep ill words from spewing out my mouth.

I silently hoped my mother prayed for our traveling mercy and safety because what I was about to do, we'd definitely needed the mercy of God and all the protection that could shield us.

One hour and a half we were cruising the Georgetown roads just an hour short of Ocean City, Maryland. I couldn't keep my mind off that even though Kyron married me, him and Pumpkin had gone behind my back and had – not one, – but two damn babies together! I hated both of them with a passion!

It had been over two years of them living together and ten years that he and I were together and that tramp still had an unshakeable obsession for *my* man. It was crystal clear to me that she had access to him 50% of the time.

Sitting in the same mini van she called a cargo van, my stomach was doing summersaults. My character had to coincide with the thoughts that ran through my mind. I didn't want to involve my kids, but I was blind with fury. In the worst way, I wanted to kill my husband and Pumpkin for continuously involving me in this love triangle. While I was losing my mind in the passenger's seat, Kyron was singing Gerald loudly:

♪ *Just because I'm wrong/It don't make you right/Why can't we make love/Instead of fuss and fight* ♪

What a song for him to continue to rewind and play. My intuition told me that he couldn't let go of the past. And now, neither could I. Perspiration was trickling down my face and I could taste the salt when the sweat dripped down on my lips. Still that taste was sweet compared to the sourness in my pit. In a twisted mental state, I glanced back at my girls and asked God to protect them as I unexpectedly reached over and spun the wheel out of control ramming us into the other lane as a tractor-trailer was coming head on.

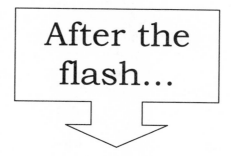

After the flash...

"Serenity, Serenity, is you with me?" I could faintly hear Medina, but the constant shaking was bringing me to.

"*Medina*," I muffled lowly. "*Where am I?*" My body was so relaxed, lying flatly. Immediately, I realized I was lying on a hospital bed. I felt a fluffy pillow underneath my neck. My breasts were free, without the support of a bra. I could feel them as I began to lift up, but was instantly guided back down by Medina.

"Let me lift your bed up," she insisted, while adjusting my bed.

That's when I noticed I had an IV attached to my right arm. That explained the tightness that I felt. My eyes were full of crust and I could barely open them up before Medina used a washcloth to clear them of mucous. The shadow behind her appeared to be Scabby.

"Scabby?" I managed to muffle out his name and clear my throat at the same time.

"I'm right here, baby." His arm came from around Medina and reached out to touch me.

It took me a moment to absorb why they seemed so distant, sad even. I tried to retrace my steps. Why in the hell was I in the hospital? I was becoming the most forgetful person, but this time I didn't remember getting high or drunk.

"What happened to me?" I asked them.

Medina began to passively rub on Scabby. I began to wonder where Kyron was. If it was as bad as they looked, how come he wasn't here to console me?

"You were in an accident, don't you recall? The van was totaled," easily came out of Medina's mouth.

I shook my head "no", but as I was tossing my head from side to side, flashbacks of me, Kyron and my girls came to me.

"My girls! My girls!" I retracted. "Where is Dalya and Tashee?"

I felt the pressure began to build in my chest. My eyes couldn't swell up any more than what they already were. What had I done?

"They were with you," Scabby sadly informed me since Medina seemed stripped of words.

"Are they okay?" I wanted so badly to rise up from that damn bed I was confined to.

"Both of them suffered broken arms, but they are home with your mom. They're okay," Scabby uneasily reported.

"Your mom doesn't want you to worry about them. She told me to tell you to just get better."

"Medina, what did I do?" I asked her, barely recollecting what took place. Then, a light bulb lit in my head. That's when I remembered taking control of the wheel doing the unthinkable with my children in the van. The pain hurt so badly. I needed a pain reliever to stop the hurting.

"How long have I been in here?"

Time was of the essence. I wondered if days, weeks, or months had past since my world came crashing around me.

"Eight days today." Medina softly informed me.

"Eight days," I said verbatim.

"You've been waking up and drifting right back out every time you get a dose of morphine."

Damn, morphine? I had to be jacked up if they were giving me morphine for pain.

The inevitable question was at the tip of my tongue: although, I didn't want to ask in fear of hearing grave news.

"Am I going to be okay?"

"Don't you always?" Scabby smiled. "What can keep you down? Not a damn thing. You's a real rider, Serenity."

I formed a half smile. My face ached and felt so tight and puffy. I wanted to see a mirror badly, but I needed to know about Kyron first. I began to wheeze and sniffle with heartbreaking tears streaming down my face.

"What about Kyron? Am I going to jail? Did I kill him?"

Medina turned to face Scabby and buried her head in his chest crying louder than I was.

"Oh, God!" I cried, with the thought of the worst. "I got him killed, didn't I?" Believing that had to be the worse pain that ever ached my entire body.

Scabby consoled Medina and tightly pulled his bottom lip inside of his mouth. Neither would answer whether or not he was dead. I assumed he was and they just didn't want to reveal that information to me.

I closed my eyes and asked, "Can you get the nurse in here to help me go to sleep again? I need her to take this pain away."

I wanted to die right there. I had to be the most horrific wife and mother a husband and kids could have. My mom had finally proven me right. I was just like my father – impulsive and regretful "after the fact". The room was so quiet with the exception of crying sounds coming from Medina and me.

I heard footsteps coming closer. I was thankful that the nurse had come to relieve me of my woes. I opened my eyes to thank her.

"Thanks, give me all--" I stopped mid sentence. It wasn't the nurse: it was Kyron! Not a bruise or a scratch on him. He was perfectly fine. I thanked God that all of us were alive, but still was angry with him.

"I'm glad you found your way back to us. For a minute I thought you decided to throw in the towel." Kyron stood before me.

The odds were always against us. Here I thought, what is the percentage of childhood sweethearts marrying and living happily ever after? Slim to fuckin' none! He was right, I had truly thrown in the towel the day I tried to hurt us. I remembered spinning the wheel out of control towards that truck because Kyron had another family. That's why I lost it. Yet, he was here in my hospital room welcoming me back amongst the living.

"Who would have known that GMC had a driver's airbag installed? That thing saved my life," he paused in deep thought, "You're one crazy woman, you know that? I thought I was the crazy one, but you got me for sure."

I had yet to tell him that Pumpkin's "foster sisters" were really their daughters. I came to the conclusion he would never be mine and just mine. He had a family with Pumpkin and she let it be known that she wasn't disappearing no matter how long she needed to wait for him. I didn't come from that flock.

"We're gonna get something to eat since Kyron is here so you two can talk alone," Medina offered.

"No, I want both of you to stay here with me. I can't trust what Kyron will do to me."

Kyron had been exposed. I was angry and didn't want to be alone with him. I almost ruined my life and my daughter's lives because I lost control of my emotions over him. Though I was concerned about his life, I didn't want him in mine any longer. The two of us never shared healthy affection for each other after he got out of jail. I wasn't right for him and he wasn't right for me. Time had gotten the best of both of us in a negative way. I should've known it wasn't going to work between us. We had forced each other into staying and lying to ourselves that we were still in love when we weren't. We were only passing time. It was now time to clean up the pile of shit we left.

Kyron was startled by my response.

"What are you talking about you don't wanna be alone with me? I'm the one that should be saying that."

I stopped leading him to believe that everything was righteous with us and I knew the truth.

"Kyron, I know that you're still seeing Pumpkin."

Quickly he responded being untruthful, "No, I'm not. It's been over between us."

"Stop it, Kyron, please! You've put me through enough. You got me back. If this is payback for me having a baby on you, you win. I surrender!"

"This was never about revenge, Serene."

"I guess it couldn't be because her kids are around the same age as Dalya. That's why you took me back. Your backyard was already piled with mounds of dirt. I've always wondered what really made you come back to me. Now I know, you felt guilty."

"You're wrong, Serenity."

"How could you and Pumpkin hide the fact that you have kids together? Is she stuck so far up your ass that she would keep this from me, to keep you? Apparently, she is. You two deserve one another."

I had him standing there speechless holding onto the window pane by the bed.

"Who told you that, she did? You gon' listen to her? C'mon, Serene. Baby, you can't leave me now."

"Yeah, I'ma listen to her because you ain't nothin' but a liar!" Even though I didn't have confirmation, I believed they were his kids.

Scabby and Medina were standing in limbo waiting to come to my rescue. I knew it was killing them to hold back what they really wanted to say.

"What a bitch will do to keep a man!" Scabby blurted out.

It didn't matter to me anymore; I was tired and burned out. This is why I didn't hide any of my feelings. I had to air out my differences.

"I've been gone, Kyron. The first time that I decided to cheat on you was the day that my heart genuinely left you. Any man you have to cheat on to seek outside affection is not worth staying with. All those years after I cheated were just out of emotion. All I wanted to do was beat the other woman in this game. When in actuality, all three of us were playing mind games with one another. I can't see myself fighting for what's not mine. I've shared you for years yet, you made me out to be this trifling ass woman and you were nothing more than a trifling-ass man! **You** molded me this way. The clay was yours to design and look at your end result. What happened to the guy that encouraged me to take on the world without fear? I'll tell what... you lost your confidence when you got busted. You let prison break you down. You weren't the same determined Kyron when you came home. You let that weak bitch make you into a complacent man and to depend on her. That's why our situation got old real fast to you. You got used to having a female do more for you than you did for yourself. Yeah, you said you wanted us to have our own, but you were selling more wolf tickets than Dame-fuckin'-Dash! I told you before I couldn't do this and I won't. I've tortured myself long enough." The strength came from my struggle. I'd beaten' myself up physically and emotionally trying to keep this man.

My eyes continued to leak and I watched as Kyron picked up the tissue box to remove a few tissues. With the tissue in his hand, he gently wiped away the secretions from the crevices of my eyes.

"That was heartfelt, but I'm not going anywhere, Serene. Those are not my kids and I'm not in love with Pumpkin."

"Playa," Scabby butted in, fed up with listening to Kyron's lies, "do yourself a favor and stop while you're ahead."

"Listen man, I'm not all up in your business so please stay out of mine. Serenity is my wife, not my sister, but my wife. I know how much y'all care for her, but I am still her husband. Ease up, ai'ight."

"Serenity, what do you want us to do?" Medina asked, ignoring him.

I sighed.

"I want you to get me a mirror so I can see if my pretty face is as fucked up as it feels."

I sensed a glimpse of hesitation in Medina's eyes.

"What?" I used my left hand to push the control buttons on the side of the bed to prop myself up further than what I was. My free arm was restrained from me lifting it. My body began to get warm and I wanted them to pull my hair up in a ponytail to take the hair off of my neck.

"Before you spazz, it's going to take some time to heal," Medina answered nervy, before the compact mirror was set before me.

"Let me see damn-it!" I cursed. I was ready for whatever at this point.

Kyron sat on the bed with me, stretching his hand out to Medina for the small mirror to place it in front of my face.

"*Aaaagh!*" I moaned. My nose was dislocated and both of my eyes were blue-black swollen and almost shut. I was hideous!

"It doesn't matter how you look right now, time heals all wounds." Medina tried to give me a glimpse of hope.

"Scabby, look at my face," I grumbled. "How can I still be a dime piece like this?"

Scabby moved to the opposite side of the bed that Kyron was on. It was time for big bro to give his words of wisdom. I knew he had something to say about me causing the accident.

"I'm not gonna dog you about this, but I will speak my peace. Don't you ever let a man send you on a suicide mission! You buck his ass first," he sincerely, declared.

I laughed within. That was Scabby, always, upfront. "Get 'em, before they get you" was his philosophy.

One thing I was thankful of, God protected us from serious injury. Unfortunately, He didn't protect my heart. It still ached from what I thought was love and as miserable as I was about my outer appearance, I was even more distressed about ending my marriage with Kyron. However, the time had come.

"Kyron, it's over! When I get out of here, I'm filing for divorce. Then, you'll be free to marry Pumpkin."

"I'm not signing nothin'," he protested early. "You need to stop worrying about me and worry about getting better so we can take care of our kids and the one coming."

*The one coming? That bitch had gotten pregnant again by him! Pumpkin had **really** hijacked my life.*

"You're just like an energizer bunny for her, huh. You just keep going and going. But with me, its one minute, two minutes, three minutes, done," I spat at him in disgust.

I put all of the thoughts of my marriage aside: it was over. It didn't matter what anyone said.

"No silly, we have another baby on the way," he said rubbing my belly like everything would be "okay".

I turned to Scabby and Medina and asked them to call for Security to get his simple ass outta my face. I wish the fuck I would have another baby by his broke ass!

Let It Burn

It was early, my first day home from the hospital, and already I was going off.

"Ella, move outta my way!" I screamed.

I couldn't believe that damn Kyron. Tell me why he hadn't removed any of his belongings from the basement? I'll tell you why, he wanted me to do it! That's exactly what I was trying to do and I wasn't nearly as calm as I had been when I was in the hospital. I had my mom's large metal trashcan in the center of the backyard where my girls loved to play, toys scattered about. That didn't stop me from tossing all of Kyron's clothes inside the can just shy of throwing a lit match to torch them. However, my mom, Ella, the savior, had jumped in my way.

"I'm not going to let you act a fool in front of them."

Them meaning, Dalya and Tashee who were standing in the doorway of the kitchen exit that lead to the balcony.

"Tell them to take their asses in the house then!" I was completely out of breath, overworking myself. "By the way, have you told Dalya about her two sisters?"

I could see my mom get tight-lipped and after a pregnant pause she responded, "You **STOP** this, this instant, Serenity! Out here acting like a damn wild woman. You can't go outside to fix the inside, honey, and if you can't fix the inside, you can just pack your things and leave my house!"

"Oh, so you gon' put me out? That's fucked up, Ella... and *in front of my kids, too?*"

Tashee wouldn't budge. However, Dalya got bold and came out further on the balcony looking down at us defending her grandmother.

"Mommy, don't talk to Mom-mom like that!"

I paused staring at the matches in my hand ready to strike every last one and it didn't matter *who* was watching.

"Lil' girl, if you don't take your lil' ass back in the house and stay in a child's place before I whip 'dat ass!"

I could see Tashee sobbing, gripping the kitchen door scared for her sister. I felt a forceful thrust and my left shoulder plunged back from my mom shoving it.

"Look at what you're teaching my grandbabies! This doesn't make any damn sense and you have a nerve to be pregnant *again*! *No, no, no more!* I'm a Christian woman. This time I won't turn the other cheek! Please don't have that baby. Come on Dalya and Tashee!" she fussed, walking up the stairs to the platform of the balcony.

Dalya hung her arms around her waist and they walked from the platform to go inside. I couldn't wait for them to do so, so I could drop every match on Kyron's clothes. Yep, and blaze those bitches right the fuck up!

I ripped off one of the matches, striking it so it could catch fire. Soon as it did, I lit the rest and dropped them down on his clothes.

"Ma'fucka!" I shouted.

I didn't even stay to watch them burn. Proudly, I strutted my ass from the backyard through the alley to the front of my house, on my way to Medina's to tell her what I'd done.

It Don't Matter

"Tell me how I should do it then?" I asked Medina and Scabby who were baffled by my plea. Scabby's forehead was frowned so much his eyebrows met making a unibrow.

"Yo, you don' lost ya fuckin' mind. You do that shit and you'll never see daylight again. At least not from this view."

"Yeah," Medina added, "I thought you were done with them. Why jeopardize your life like that?"

"No, the question is why did they play me like that? Now, do you have my back or what? I only need a ride. When we get there I'll throw the Molotov cocktail in the bay window of Pumpkin's house and afterwards we can floor it!"

Medina tugged at her man.

"Bitch, don' lost her mind haven't she, Scabby?"

"I know 'dat's right," he agreed.

Both of them stood there with stupid expressions on their faces, not helping me at all.

"Serenity, what if her kids are there?" Medina asked, for the kid's safety. I don't give a rat's ass if they were. The hell with them too!

"Don't insult me, Medina! Did that bitch care enough about her own kids to reveal them? What bitch would deny her kids for a man? I don't even know how that slipped by me! I know I wasn't that caught up! They got that, though! *Hmmm, hmmp*! And, you wonder why I want all of them dead?" The hurt crippled my thoughts.

"Uh oh, you gon' to hell for that one. I'm done with it," Medina said, abandoning me.

Scabby came closer to me and with a magnitude of feeling, embraced me.

"You should thank that man for rejecting you. He did you a favor. When you met him, he didn't have a pot to piss in or a window to throw it out of. He came a long way from Food Stamps. You motivated that man to get money."

I couldn't control myself and pointlessly I burst out in tears. I wanted to laugh at Scabby's silly remark and I'm sure that was his aim, but I couldn't. Instead, I acted out. My feet pounded the floor in a childish fit.

"Come on, Serenity, you're stronger than this," he insisted.

"I understand, but it's impossible to ignore the facts," I said, in my defense. And, that's when he finally pulled back from me.

We parted to the love seat in their living room. I stood, but Medina took a seat.

"Sit down, Serenity. You might ass well get comfortable. You don't have a damn place to be.

Lemme drop some of this knowledge on you. You were tired of Kyron anyway, right?" Scabby's elbows plummeted deep in his thighs.

"Sort of," I responded. Although, I secretly wished things did get better between us. "Well, not really. I just wanted him to get back on the grind. His money got too low for me. That's when I started buggin'."

"See that's what I don't understand. You've been through hell with him and Tomiere, and yet, you still want to live that life when you know what comes with it."

Medina nodded distantly.

"I don't know if it's necessarily like that. What girl in her right mind wouldn't love a thick-dick-hood nigga with swag makin' that paper? He could get it by any means; he just has to share his impressive world with me. I love a thug nigga. The game breeds hustlers and hustle bunnies. I'ma hustle bunny 'til I die."

"Girl, you need to quit it!" Medina laughed at my opinion.

"I'm sorry, boo-boo, but you know what I'm sayin'." I wasn't trying to be unnecessarily disrespectful. "Shit, I stopped feeling unwanted and ashamed a long time ago about my pitfalls as a hustle bunny: if that's what you're asking. Some things come with the game; you know that. Luckily, you haven't endured that, but it won't be long for somebody tries to run up in this spot. Especially, envious niggas who think Scabby's comin' off." Regardless of what Medina thought, she was pretty much in the same predicament. In fact, worse. Her man was still in the game. "I mean, but you do still go through what most hustle bunnies do… dealing with a cheatin' man. I can ask you if you're tired of that. Na'mean, but I won't. 'Cause like you said Medina, 'sometimes you have to put up with certain things'. Some things you can deal with, some things you can't. I can't and I won't deal with what Kyron has done. Especially, when ain't no perks in it. Shit, I can't remember the last time he dropped a grand in my hands. And that, used to come easy! Kyron's too complacent and useless to me now. Trust that, it doesn't mean I won't deal with another man's shortcomings. "Cause, I'm sure he'll have some. In spite of this, he may be worth fixing. Just like its niggas that are stuck in the game, so are females. I'm one of them. Kyron should've never introduced me to it."

"Ride for yours, baby!" Scabby smiled.

"Me, I can live without it. On the real though, who you should've fixed was JaQuill and Jermaine. It seems like you let that ride. Took it on the chin, huh? I know you ain't that committed to the game," Medina redeemed.

"Oh, don't worry. I got 'em. I'ma fix both of them up when I contact Detective Talbert with their information."

That was undoubtedly the truth. On the strength of Kyron, I didn't rat JaQuill out, but since he wanted to play me, I was gonna retaliate.

"Let's get back to what I was saying in the beginning of our conversation. 'Cause y'all missed the real point. For real… *y'all don't think it's a good idea for me to set that bitch's house on fire?*"

"HELL NO! How did you find out where she lives anyway?" Medina inquired, curiously.

"Urs."

"Keep fuckin' 'round with Urs. She gon' have you hemmed up," Scabby heaved.

"She ain't lied to me yet though, that's for sure," I said, taking up for Urs.

"Back to the issue, you know ya big bro ain't wit' snitchin', but those niggas deserve the time that's gonna be thrown their way. As for Kyron, let it go. Skeet is try'na holla at you anyway and my dude got loot. A straight balla, just how you like 'em."

"Say word, nucka!" I smiled.

Epilogue

It was six months ago when I was in the hospital after damn near killing my husband, my two kids and myself. I am pleased to report that as fucked up as I thought my situation was, living is in no comparison. Not that I was trying to kill myself, but my impulsive behavior, jeopardized our lives. I had to get my shit together, not just for my kids, but also for my own sake. Over time my face did heal. Horribly, I am stuck with a nasty scar right on the inner arch of my nose, *but I'm still pretty*. It's a reminder everyday when I look in the mirror of how foolish I was. I am back working full-time as a hustle bunny for my new friend, Skeet. Yep, I sure did!

For the last and *hopefully* the final time, I moved out of my mother's house into an affordable condo and Skeet is a frequent visitor since he pays the financial note. Ella cried tears of joy and sadness when I packed up my things to move out. Just as I was about to get Dalya and

Tashee things, her tears of joy quickly dried up. She wasn't havin' that.

"I wish the hell you would! My grands can't live with you until you get it together!" were her exact comments.

There weren't any words for me to say to rebut her underlying principle of me as a mother. I still needed to clean up my act. Even more important, I realized that I wasn't ready to take on the full responsibility of being a mother. Now, I sincerely understood what Urs meant. So, I get my girls every other weekend and the weekends they're not with me, they are with their fathers. That was a start for me, seeing as though, I still wanted to party.

I tackled one of my main fears when I aborted my only son. That was yet another troubling decision I had to make. What was helpful was the fact that the hospital was giving me morphine at will. I wasn't willing to chance my baby being an addict. Then another contributing factor was my mother begged me not to bring another child in this world for her to raise so, I didn't. I couldn't see myself trying to raise three kids on my own anyhow; I just couldn't. I know that I'ma get punished and the consequences are gonna weigh heavier than the burden that is already on me. Yet, I know what's best for me. That's all that matters. I know my limitations.

Oh yeah, I'm sure you wanna know... I didn't reconcile with Kyron. In fact, our divorce hearing is today. We haven't had civil conversation since I was in the hospital. Yes, before you ask, he did go back to Pumpkin and those are truly his kids. You didn't believe him, did you? 'Cause I didn't. But that's Pumpkin's headache because Dalya came home from a short visit with her dad, and Kyron had our daughter around another hoodrat who's after his magic stick. Thinking he still got it, when he don't. I guess that was the other chick that was on his voicemail, who knows. Leave it to children, they'll sho' 'nuff tell it. Even though, Kyron is Pumpkin's worry, I'ma still get that bitch when I see her!

To me, it's always about winning and I felt like I won when I struck big time with Skeet. He has five times more money than Kyron had when he was in the game. My new man got property, cars, timeshares, stocks and more investments. That's why when I pull up in this luxury Cayenne Porsche all of them gon' hate. Wait to big face see me in this. I'ma laugh all in that bitch's face 'cause Kyron ain't giving her nothin' but a wet ass. That's all her dumb ass wants anyway. Stupid slut. I can't see me being a woman who foots all the bills, carrying a man. Hell no! That's why God made Adam first. If it were meant for a woman to lead, he would've made Eve the head, but He didn't.

I'd rather live this new life any day! It ain't for all women though, only extra chicks like me. ☺

() () () () ()

As far as, JaQuill and Jermaine, even though I contacted the Detective with their information, I got word from Urs that they still doin' them. I tried to help the Police out – to help me out, – but those bastards still ain't done their fuckin' job! Then, Urs told me JaQuill raped one of her girl's and they hadn't caught him yet. It's a damn shame! Once a rapist, always a rapist!

▽▽▽▽

Scabby finally buckled down and asked Medina to be his wife. Don't mean a damn thing, but layaway if you ask me. He's still beatin' the block out from the concrete, just doing him. That's why they haven't set an official date yet. One great thing though, they are expecting a baby! Yep, Medina is finally going to go through with it this time. Of the two abortions she had, she hadn't witnessed one until the doctor agreed that she could witness mine (my suggestion). I didn't have to cry because Medina cried enough tears for both of us and vowed that she'd never have an abortion again. *Ain't that a bitch?* I bet if Scabby knew that sooner, he would've had her at abortion clinics all over Delaware to witness how harsh it is when someone is aborting a life.

I'm really happy for both of them and I still envy the relationship that they share. They may have their ups and downs, but they love each other! True love is hard to find nowadays. Medina says if she has a girl, she's going to name her Serenity and maybe this time someone will uphold the name, with her ig-nant ass.

≶ ≶ ≶ ≶ ≶

Urs, she's still my down-ass chick. She's real, that's what I love about her. When I went to her to see if she knew anything about Skeet, she said, "No, but I can get to know him if you want. If he got product, he got me."

♠ ♠ ♠ ♠ ♠

As for me, I'ma see where this relationship with Skeet leads me. So far, I haven't cheated on him. Not yet, and don't plan to... not unless he cheats on me. *You know the rules!* Tomiere tried to test that, but he's old news to me. Anyway, while Skeet's money is right, I'ma hold true. I bet he betta not go to jail though. If he does, I'ma get him for all the cash I can and bounce on his ass!

Why you shaking your head? I ain't no damn role model.

Other Titles
by
KaShamba Williams

- Blinded
- Grimey
- Driven
- At the Courts Mercy
- Around the Way Girls 2 (Anthology)
- Girls In Da Hood 2 (Anthology)
- Girls In Da Hood 3 (Anthology)
- Even Sinners Have Souls (Anthology)

PTE Order Form

QTY	TITLE	PRICE
	Around The Way Girls 2 by KaShamba Williams, LaJill Hunt & Thomas Long	$14.95
	At The Courts Mercy by KaShamba Williams	$14.95
	Dirty Dawg by Unique J. Shannon	$14.95
	Doe Boy by G. Rell	$14.95
	DRIVEN by KaShamba Williams	$14.95
	Girls From Da Hood 2 by K. Williams, Nikki Turner & Joy	$14.95
	Girls From Da Hood 3 by K.Williams, Mark Anthony, Madam K	$14.95
	Hittin' Numbers by Unique J. Shannon	$14.95
	In My Peace I Trust by Brittney Davis	$14.95
	Latin Heat by BP Love	$14.95
	One Love 'Til I Die by Tony Trusell	$14.95
	Mind Games by KaShamba Williams	$14.95
	Stiletto 101 by Lenaise Meyeil	$14.95
	The Tommy Good Story by Leondrei Prince	$14.95
	Thug's Passion by Tracy Gray	$14.95
	Victim of The Ghetto by Joel Rhodes	$14.95
	Platinum Teen Series	
	Dymond In The Rough	$6.99
	The AB-solute Truth	$6.99
	Runaway	$6.99
	Best Kept Secret	$6.99
	Total:	

Please include shipping and handling fee of $2.50.
Forms of payment accepted – money orders, credit card,
Paypal, debit cards, postal stamps and Institutional checks.
Please allow 5-7 business days for books to arrive.
Precioustymes Entertainment
229 Governors Place, #138
Bear, DE 19701

Coming Soon!

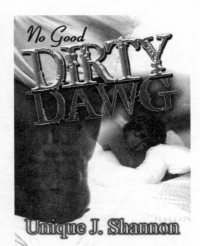

July 2007   September 2007

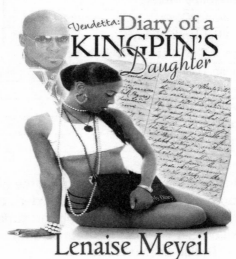

Searching for "safe" Urban Fiction books for your
10-15 year olds to read?
Try the Platinum Teen Series.
No explicit language or explicit content.

PTE is the 1st Urban Fiction Publishing
Company to delivery a teen series of this kind!!

PTE Order Form

QTY	TITLE	PRICE
	Around The Way Girls 2 by KaShamba Williams, LaJill Hunt & Thomas Long	$14.95
	At The Courts Mercy by KaShamba Williams	$14.95
	Dirty Dawg by Unique J. Shannon	$14.95
	Doe Boy by G. Rell	$14.95
	DRIVEN by KaShamba Williams	$14.95
	Girls From Da Hood 2 by K. Williams, Nikki Turner & Joy	$14.95
	Girls From Da Hood 3 by K.Williams, Mark Anthony, Madam K	$14.95
	Hittin' Numbers by Unique J. Shannon	$14.95
	In My Peace I Trust by Brittney Davis	$14.95
	Latin Heat by BP Love	$14.95
	One Love 'Til I Die by Tony Trusell	$14.95
	Mind Games by KaShamba Williams	$14.95
	Stiletto 101 by Lenaise Meyeil	$14.95
	The Tommy Good Story by Leondrei Prince	$14.95
	Thug's Passion by Tracy Gray	$14.95
	Victim of The Ghetto by Joel Rhodes	$14.95
	Platinum Teen Series	
	Dymond In The Rough	$6.99
	The AB-solute Truth	$6.99
	Runaway	$6.99
	Best Kept Secret	$6.99
	Total:	

Please include shipping and handling fee of $2.50.
Forms of payment accepted – money orders, credit card,
Paypal, debit cards, postal stamps and Institutional checks.
Please allow 5-7 business days for books to arrive.

Precioustymes Entertainment
229 Governors Place, #138
Bear, DE 19701

www.precioustymes.com

Coming Soon!

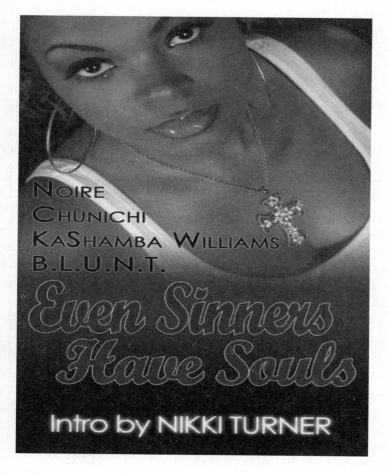

Christmas 2007

PTE Order Form

QTY	TITLE	PRICE
	Around The Way Girls 2 by KaShamba Williams, LaJill Hunt & Thomas Long	$14.95
	At The Courts Mercy by KaShamba Williams	$14.95
	Dirty Dawg by Unique J. Shannon	$14.95
	Doe Boy by G. Rell	$14.95
	DRIVEN by KaShamba Williams	$14.95
	Girls From Da Hood 2 by K. Williams, Nikki Turner & Joy	$14.95
	Girls From Da Hood 3 by K.Williams, Mark Anthony, Madam K	$14.95
	Hittin' Numbers by Unique J. Shannon	$14.95
	In My Peace I Trust by Brittney Davis	$14.95
	Latin Heat by BP Love	$14.95
	One Love 'Til I Die by Tony Trusell	$14.95
	Mind Games by KaShamba Williams	$14.95
	Stiletto 101 by Lenaise Meyeil	$14.95
	The Tommy Good Story by Leondrei Prince	$14.95
	Thug's Passion by Tracy Gray	$14.95
	Victim of The Ghetto by Joel Rhodes	$14.95
	Platinum Teen Series	
	Dymond In The Rough	$6.99
	The AB-solute Truth	$6.99
	Runaway	$6.99
	Best Kept Secret	$6.99
	Total:	

Please include shipping and handling fee of $2.50.
Forms of payment accepted – money orders, credit card,
Paypal, debit cards, postal stamps and Institutional checks.
Please allow 5-7 business days for books to arrive.

Precioustymes Entertainment
229 Governors Place, #138
Bear, DE 19701

www.precioustymes.com

Black & Nobel Books
&
Distribution

**1411 W. Erie Avenue
Philadelphia, PA**

(215) 965-1559

**www.myspace.com/blackandnobelbooks
www.blackandnobel.com**

Still Rising in Numbers!

Blinded

Grimey

www.triplecrownpublications.com

Follow Nasir's Story

Finish with the Sequel
At the Courts Mercy

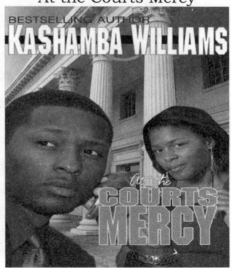

www.urbanbooks.net

A story based on the life of alleged "Ghetto Boys" leader – Joel "Dolo" Rhodes as told to Tasha Wilson.

This book is based on a compelling journey of love, hate, trust, betrayal, loyalty, envy, and honor. It is based on the life of Joel a.k.a (Dolo) Rhodes a man with many labels. While his heart yearned for god his soul was lost to the streets. He became a victim of his own game by the very hands of those he once protectively overshadowed.

www.remembermeproductions.com